Y OU have a shrewish tongue, my girl," said Jonas. "Beware lest it lead you into trouble."

Charity flung back her head and laughed aloud. "Tis not my tongue has provoked most trouble of late, Jonas. Yours could have wrought your death had Darrell not shown you mercy."

Jonas's face, already pale with anger, went whiter yet, and his lips twisted venomously. All the humiliation of that duel by the river, all his overmastering jealousy and hatred of Darrell Conyngton, swept over him with renewed force.

"It is a mercy he will live to regret. I tell you, cousin, a day will come when he shall wish with all his heart that he had slain me while it was in his power to do so. I do not forget, nor will I be content until I see his damned Conyngton pride humbled and trodden into the dust. Before God I swear it!"

Suddenly a chill of foreboding crept into Charity's heart.

Fawcett Crest Books
by Sylvia Thorpe:

SYLVIA THORPE

Fair Shine the Day

A FAWCETT CREST BOOK

Fawcett Publications, Inc., Greenwich, Connecticut

FAIR SHINE THE DAY

THIS BOOK CONTAINS THE COMPLETE TEXT OF
THE ORIGINAL HARDCOVER EDITION.

A Fawcett Crest Book reprinted by arrangement with Hutch-
inson Publishing Group.

© J. S. THIMBLETHORPE 1964
ALL RIGHTS RESERVED

ISBN 0-449-23229-8

Printed in the United States of America

10 9 8 7 6 5 4 3 2 1

Fair the day shine as it shone on my childhood—
Fair shine the day on the house with open door;
Birds come and cry there and twitter in the chimney—
But I go for ever and come again no more.

Robert Louis Stevenson

Fair Shine the Day

Book One

1

Charity, the Child

The May morning was clear but cold, the sky a delicate, cloud-flecked blue, a stiff breeze tugging at the young leaves and shaking the spring flowers in the prim beds of Jonathan Shenfield's garden. It was very early, too early for any but the servants to be astir in the Moat House as Charity Shenfield crept down the backstairs and along the stone-flagged passage which skirted the kitchen quarters. The door at its far end was her goal, a door which opened on to the yard lying between houses and stables, and from which escape into the park and the open countryside was a simple matter.

She held her breath as she tiptoed along the passage, for although there was little reason why she should not walk abroad in the early morning, and no one in the kitchens had any real authority to stop her, she knew that if she were discovered there would be exclamations and

11

questions, and the magic of this perfect morning spoiled beyond repair.

She reached the door at last and drew it softly open. The yard was deserted, and, catching up her skirts, she fled across to the gate which already stood wide, crossed the gravelled drive leading to the front of the house, and soon reached the rough grassland of the park. She ran until she could run no farther and then halted, gasping for breath, beneath the spreading branches of an oak tree. She leaned against the great, rough trunk, arms outspread and head thrown back, as still as some wild creature yet revelling in her moment of complete freedom.

Charity was thirteen years old, and her name had been bestowed upon her as a constant reminder of her worldly estate, for, orphaned at birth, she was wholly dependent upon the charity of her father's elder brother, Jonathan Shenfield. He was a just man, who had never blamed the child for that which was no fault of hers, but her unfortunate circumstances, coupled with the fact that she was half French, had inevitably left their mark upon her childhood, setting her apart from his own three children with whom she had been reared. These facts, however, seldom weighed heavily upon her, and never less than on that bright May morning in the year 1641.

When she had recovered her breath she moved away from the oak tree and walked on, slowly now that there was no longer any fear of pursuit. She had no particular destination in mind. It was enough merely to be alone and out of doors, free for a time from the bullying of her cousin Jonas, three years her senior, and the indifference of Beth and Sarah, his two sisters; from the monotonous round of lessons and domestic duties against which her whole being so often cried out in silent rebellion. There might be a reckoning to pay later, but she could not be still while happiness and excitement were bubbling like spring-water within her. This was the day to which she had looked forward the whole winter long.

She came at length to the stream which on this side formed the boundary of her uncle's land, and beyond which, stretching far in every direction, lay the estate of Sir Darrell Conyngton. His family had been squires of those parts for generations, and their imprint lay everywhere upon the countryside. The village of Conyngton St John a mile or so away in the next valley took its name from them, and their great mansion, which crowned the hill between the village and the Moat House, was named, simply and proudly, Conyngton.

Charity hitched up her skirts, picked her way precariously across the turbulent brook by means of two large stones and a rotting, half-submerged tree-trunk, and scrambled up the muddy bank beyond. Here the wooded hillside rose steeply, but the narrow path which wound its way upwards between the trees was as familiar to her as the formal walks of her uncle's garden. The two neighbouring families had been on friendly terms for many years, but ironically enough, it had been left to Charity to forge the first really close bond between them. Of all the Shenfields, she was the most frequent and most welcome visitor to the manor—a fact which her cousin Jonas found supremely irritating.

From the far edge of the woods, where they bordered the broad park where deer grazed, Conyngton itself could be seen, a splendid house built in the old Queen's time to replace an earlier, smaller manor. It stood crowning the hill-top, its tall chimneys and many-gabled roof outlined against the clear spring sky, graceful leaded windows

13

flashing in the morning sun. Terraced gardens were at its feet, great trees and smooth lawns, statues and arbours and formal flower-beds, the whole surrounded by a high brick wall with a square, arched gatehouse. A stately mansion, reflecting the wealth and pride of the family that dwelt in it. "As proud as a Conyngton" was an adage well known in the surrounding countryside. Most people accepted it, for it was a pride without arrogance. Only a few, like young Jonas Shenfield, and a few malcontents in nearby Plymouth, resented it, and muttered against it among themselves.

Charity loved Conyngton in all its aspects, but this view of it, when after the steep climb through the woods the beautiful house came suddenly in sight, was one of which she never tired. She lingered for a while, looking at the manor, knowing that, early though it was, there would already be a bustle of preparation within its walls. There was rejoicing at Conyngton that fair spring day, for the only son of the house was bringing home his bride.

To Charity, young Darrell Conyngton was the most important person in the world, and had been so ever since the day, now six years past, when he had first rescued her from Jonas's cruel bullying, and so founded a relationship which puzzled many people and irked Jonas himself beyond measure. It was a strangely assorted friendship, between the Shenfields' despised, half-foreign little kinswoman and Sir Darrell Conyngton's son and heir, but it had had an immeasurable influence on Charity's hitherto rather bleak life. When it was seen that Sir Darrell himself looked kindly upon her, and that his wife had taken the little girl under her wing, it was tacitly acknowledged at Conyngton and its immediate surroundings that Charity Shenfield was no longer altogether unimportant.

The girl herself, provided for by her uncle from a sense of duty, and dutifully grateful, soon became devoted to the squire and his lady, but it was always to young Darrell that her strongest loyalty and deepest affection were given. He was four years older than she, growing into manhood while she was still in the schoolroom, and yet time had served merely to strengthen the bond between them, until he looked upon her almost as the sister he lacked.

Their friendship was interrupted only when Sir Darrell, deeming it time that his son saw something of the world, sent him to London to spend some time at Court before going on to Kent to make the marriage which had long been arranged for him. He had been gone from Conyngton for more than a year, but now at last his long-awaited return was at hand, and that he brought a wife with him troubled Charity not at all. The bride was not a great deal older than herself, and she was happily confident that in Alison Conyngton she would find a companion of her own age and sex with whom she had far more in common than with either of her cousins.

After a while she walked on across the park, away from the manor and towards the road that lead to the village. Some ten minutes later she passed through the great, stone-pillared gateway in the wall bounding the park, and as she went down the hill caught a glimpse of the roof and chimneys of the empty Dower House among the trees on her right. A short way farther on, the road curved sharply round the shoulder of the hill, and the village itself lay in full view below.

It was in its own way as fair a prospect as the proud mansion on the hill, its thatched cottages clustered about a green opposite which the little church of St. John lifted its square tower among dark yew trees. Beyond the church, on the far side of the small river that wandered down the valley, a bright flash of reflected sunlight betrayed the mill's great water-wheel, while to the right the long, low, thatch-roofed inn fronted the old stone bridge and the road that led to Plymouth. With a fresh burst of excited energy Charity went running down the hill, and so overtook a stalwart youth in homespun who was walking briskly in the same direction, a dog at his heels. He glanced round at the sound of her approach and she recognized Diccon Bramble, the innkeeper's eldest son. He halted and grinned at her, touching the lock of tow-coloured hair which fell untidily across his forehead.

"Good morrow to 'ee, Miss Charity," he greeted her. "You be early abroad."

She stooped to fondle the dog which was fawning about her. "Oh, I could not lie abed on such a morning, Diccon," she replied gaily, "and today of all days!"

"Aye," he agreed, nodding, " 'tis a great day for Conyngton! There'll be little enough work done, I'm thinking, and rare merrymaking in the village to greet Master Darrell and his lady!"

"We have been bidden to Conyngton to dine. Sir Darrell gives a feast to welcome them," Charity remarked, walking on beside him. "Oh, it will be good to have Darrell here again! He has been away so long, but now Lady Conyngton says that he and his wife will remain in Devonshire."

"Happen they will, Miss Charity! There be trouble up to Lunnon, so 'tis said."

"Trouble?" Charity turned to look at him, frowning. "What manner of trouble?"

He shrugged and shook his head. To one who had

16

never travelled more than five miles from his native village, London might have belonged to another world. The dissension between King and Parliament, the impeachment of the King's chief Minister, even the presence in the north of an invading Scottish army, were but remote and puzzling rumours, of far less import than the number of new lambs or the chance of a good harvest.

"There be talk to Plymouth, seemingly," he said vaguely after a moment. "A pedlar were by yesterday who said some there speak hot against the King."

Charity walked on in silence, her frown deepening. She was only a child, but she possessed a lively and inquiring mind, and Diccon's words recalled certain things she had heard her cousin Jonas say. Jonas went often to Plymouth. His mother came of a prosperous merchant family there, and her two brothers, who had no sons of their own, liked to have the boy visit them. It was understood that he would come into a handsome inheritance from them some day, and his father made no objection to his learning something of their business. That he learned other things also Jonas did not disclose, and aired his knowledge and his views only to Charity. He disliked and despised his little orphaned kinswoman, but at least she would listen to him, which his own sisters would not, nor babble everything he said to his parents.

From Jonas, Charity had learned of grievances against the tax commonly called Ship Money, and against the fines for not attending church; of the war with Scotland and the King's determination to rule without Parliament; and she had become familiar with the name, often repeated and always abused, of the Earl of Strafford, the King's trusted Minister, now upon trial for his life. Jonas's information was frequently inaccurate and always coloured

17

with the prejudices of those from whom he culled it, but she had learned enough dimly to realize that all was not as well with the world as might be supposed from the pleasant placidity of life in their own quiet corner of Devonshire. Now for the first time it occurred to her that these distant troubles might one day reach out to touch her own life and the lives of those dearest to her. A vague foreboding settled upon her, dimming for a moment the bright promise of the day.

The mood was a transient one. Diccon had already abandoned the topic in favour of one of more immediate interest, and was talking of the preparations made in the village to celebrate the homecoming of the squire's heir with his bride. It was a great occasion, for Sir Darrell and his lady had but the one child, and though the marriage itself had taken place the previous autumn at the bride's home in Kent, it was only now that Conyngton had an excuse to make merry. All the neighbouring gentry had been bidden to the feast at the manor, while for humbler folk there would be music and dancing on the village green, and ample food and drink of Sir Darrell's providing. It was an occasion for rejoicing in which gentle and simple alike would share, and Charity's spirits, always buoyant, rose again as she listened.

"I wonder," she said, half to herself, "what it is like for Mrs Conyngton to be coming thus among strangers, so far from her own home and family. Do you suppose she is as curious about us as we are about her?"

Diccon scratched his head, for this was going a trifle too deep for him, but after a few seconds volunteered the information that some folk thought it a pity Master Darrell had not wed a Devonshire maid instead of a "foreigner" from another county. Then he broke off abruptly, remembering belatedly that his companion's mother had been a foreigner, not merely to Devonshire, but to England itself, but Charity did not seem to notice his confusion. She went on in the same reflective tone:

"*I* think it would be exciting to travel to places far away. I should like to go to London, and to France. To Normandy, where my mother was born. Were I a boy I *would* go, as soon as I were grown!" She drew a deep breath, her dark eyes sparkling as she warmed to her theme. "I would rise in the world, and make my fortune, and be free to do just as I wished. Oh, anything is possible if one is a man! A woman can do nothing unless she has great wealth or great beauty, and I have neither. I *wish* I had been born a boy!"

Diccon grinned at her, not fully comprehending the wish, but willing to please because he had known her all her life and in his own way was fond of her. Charity sighed. It was not Diccon she wanted to talk to, but Darrell, who always laughed with her but never at her, and who understood and sympathized with the restlessness which sometimes drove her into open rebellion against her lot. Darrell, too, would explain to her these strange and frightening rumours which Jonas brought with him from Plymouth, and of which even the stolid Diccon was now becoming aware. Ignorant though she was of the rights and wrongs of that tremendous quarrel, Charity yet knew instinctively that Jonas painted only one aspect of the picture, and that all he said was influenced by his own jealous, discontented nature.

In the village, when they reached it, people were going about their normal tasks, but there was an air of eager expectancy which was unmistakable. Charity parted from Diccon at the door of the Conyngton Arms—for he, too,

19

had work awaiting him—and then sat for a while on the low parapet of the bridge, looking now at the sparkling stream below, and now at the pleasant scene around her. The bright flowers in the cottage gardens, the blossoming fruit trees scattered throughout the village, the fresh young green of woodland and meadow clothing the surrounding hills, formed a picture of such rural serenity that it was hard to realize that only a few miles away to the north lay country of a very different character, the wild, lonely, haunted expanse of Dartmoor, while to the south the sea beat tirelessly against the unyielding coast. Sometimes Charity felt smothered in this gentle valley, and irresistibly drawn toward either the savage moor or the restless sea, but today a quiet contentment possessed her. Darrell was coming home.

She became aware at length of the swift passage of time, and, jumping down from the parapet, set off for home. She made what haste she could, but by the time she arrived there the house, which when she left it had worn a shuttered and sleeping air, was now clearly awake, and its inhabitants going about the business of the day.

She halted, guiltily aware of her own untidiness. She had dressed hurriedly, in an old stuff gown and stout shoes, and the latter were now caked with mud which had found its way also on to the skirt of her dress, while her hair, hastily bound up, was now falling about her face and shoulders. Clearly it would be prudent to restore some order to her appearance before entering the house.

She had approached from a direction different to that by which she had set out, and was now close to all that was left of the moat which gave the house its name. This was no more than a broad pool, flanked on the side nearest the house by an ancient, crumbling wall which ended in the tower of a half-ruined gatehouse. A pair of swans dwelt there, and fish glided beneath the lily-pads which dotted its surface. Charity wiped the mud from her shoes on the lush grass and then knelt by the pool, leaning over to use the still water as a mirror while she bound up her thick black hair.

The face gazing back at her from the pool confirmed her own statement that she lacked beauty. She had heard that Marguerite, her mother, had been lovely in her own dark, outlandish way, but if this were true she had bequeathed none of her good looks to her daughter except for a clear, olive-tinted complexion. Marguerite herself, had she lived to see her child grow up, would have recognized that aquiline face with its broad forehead and firm chin, the wide, well-shaped mouth, and the dark eyes deep-set beneath slanting, somewhat heavy brows. It looked down from many a family portrait in the small château in Normandy which had been her home until she fled from it to marry Robert Shenfield.

In Conyngton St John, however, among her fair-haired, blue-eyed cousins, Charity's looks set her immediately apart, while there was that in her nature which made the differences between them even more apparent. Not for her the docile obedience, the preoccupation with gentle, feminine pursuits which characterized Beth and Sarah. Jonathan Shenfield and Elizabeth, his wife, finding themselves at a loss, ruled her with a strict hand, for they saw in her the lamentable wildness which had prompted her father to disgrace his family and later carry off a foreign bride, and which within a year of his marriage had brought him to a violent and untimely end. The fact that iron discipline had in no way restrained the father did not deter them from using it upon the child.

A large stone hurtled suddenly past Charity's shoulder, and the reflection shattered and vanished as water splashed violently into her face and over her clothes. She dashed a hand across her eyes and swung round to see Jonas a few feet away. He had approached unheard across the grass and now stood, feet wide-planted and arms akimbo, grinning at her discomfiture.

"Cease staring so fondly at your own image, coz," he said with a sneer. "You have little enough cause for vanity."

She looked at him with scorn and dislike. "Perhaps I have," she retorted, "but that is better than a fair face and a faint heart. It was not *I* who shrank from mounting the new horse my uncle purchased from Sir Darrell."

Jonas flushed scarlet with rage. He was a handsome boy—all the Shenfields except Charity possessed more than a common degree of good looks—but he was not blessed with a great deal of physical courage. He tried to conceal this fact with an air of bravado, but had the uneasy feeling that he deceived nobody, and it was therefore all the more galling that his young cousin possessed so much of the hardihood he lacked. He still writhed in retrospect at the memory of a day the previous summer when Charity had climbed the ruined gatehouse tower and poised unconcernedly on its topmost point careless of the dizzy drop to the moat below, while he, attempting to follow her, had become petrified with terror less than a third of the way up, and clung there, sick and trembling, until rescued by one of the serving-men. That Charity had been severely punished for the escapade was small consolation for his own humiliation.

Most of all he resented the terms on which she stood with the Conyngtons. Jonas would have liked very much to be free of the manor, as Charity was, and to call the squire's son his friend, but Darrell had never troubled to hide his contempt for the younger boy. Who was Charity, the penniless, half-foreign orphan, to be on terms of familiarity with the great folk of the neighbourhood while he received no more than common civility? He could see that this morning she was in high spirits, and as he had no difficulty in guessing the cause, his next words were charged with even more jealousy than usual.

"Are you prinking yourself because Darrell Conyngton comes home today? Spare your pains! He brings a bride with him, and rumour has it she is more than passing fair."

This shot went wide. Charity, half sitting, half kneeling on the grass, regarded him blankly. Of course Darrell's wife was beautiful. It was unthinkable that she should be anything else.

"What is that to me? If you think my looks are likely to matter to her, any more than they have ever mattered to him, your wits must have gone a-begging!"

"Yours also, cousin, if you look to have matters stand now between you as they always did. Think you that after a year at Court, Darrell will be willing to let a silly child plague him?"

"I am not a silly child!" she cried indignantly, but took the precaution of getting to her feet before adding triumphantly: "And if I were he would still prefer my company to that of a pretty popinjay who is naught but soft plumage and a loud voice."

Jonas uttered an exclamation of fury and made a threatening movement towards her, but she darted past him and fled in the direction of the house. He pounded after her, but Charity could run like a deer and by the time he burst into the big, stone-flagged hall she was already halfway up the staircase at its farther end. From that vantage point she looked down at him, made a derisive grimace, and vanished in the direction of the bedchamber she shared with Beth and Sarah.

2

Shadow Across England

Except at prayers, Charity did not see Jonas again until they were about to depart for Conyngton, and then he was in the hall with his parents when she and Beth came down the stairs. Sarah, at nine years old, was too young to be included in the party.

Mrs Shenfield looked with an appraising yet satisfied eye at her handsome son and plump, pretty daughter, but then her glance passed on to her niece, and satisfaction abruptly faded. Since this was an important occasion she had chosen Charity's dress with more care than she usually bestowed on the girl's clothes, but the rich, strong colours which would have flattered her dark complexion were not, in Mrs Shenfield's opinion, suited either to her age or her station in life. Elizabeth had compromised by choosing amber-yellow taffeta, but was still not happy at the result.

Charity was as tall and thin as a colt, she thought impatiently—not seeing that she possessed also a colt's swift grace—and her mane of black hair so straight and heavy that it refused all efforts to coax it into curls. Had the choice been left to Elizabeth, Charity would have remained at home with Sarah, but to go to the manor without her would deeply offend the Conyngtons.

They made the journey in the great, lumbering coach, with Jonas and his father riding beside it. Jonas was in an exceedingly ill humour. Disliking Darrell Conyngton intensely, he could see in his return no cause for celebration, and would have avoided the festivities if he could. Darrell outmatched him in all things, in wealth, in rank, and in physical prowess, enjoying in addition a popularity which Jonas could never hope to command, and Jonas was in consequence bitterly jealous.

They were among the first arrivals at the manor, but the servant who conducted them up the Grand Staircase to the Long Gallery informed them that Master Darrell and his wife were already there, having lain the previous night at an inn only a few miles away.

Charity's eagerness and excitement were now so great that she found it difficult to walk demurely and quietly in her lowly position at the extreme rear of the little group, behind Jonas and Beth, who were in turn preceded by their parents. As they entered the Long Gallery, that splendid apartment which ran almost the entire width of the house, with a row of tall, embrasured windows along one side, she stood on tiptoe and craned her neck to catch a first glimpse of Darrell.

The square and his family were grouped about the nearer of the two fireplaces, Lady Conyngton seated in a big armchair while her waiting-woman hovered unobtrusively in the background. Her ladyship had been an invalid ever since the birth of her only child, and ill health had so ravaged her looks that she appeared far older than her years, but today a great happiness showed in her sweet, worn face. Her husband stood beside her, a tall man with lean, strong features, the firm chin masked by a small, pointed beard, long hair falling in ordered curls across the lace collar of his black velvet doublet. He was a commanding figure, but Charity had eyes only for the youth at his side.

The younger Darrell was very like his father, tall and long-limbed, with the hazel eyes and tawny Conyngton hair—gold-brown with more than a hint of red in it—which were a family characteristic, but in his face there showed also much of his mother's charm. Charity, studying him as she approached, thought that he had changed a good deal during his absence. He looked so much older and more self-assured than she remembered that for the first time she was conscious of the four years' difference in their ages and the even wider gulf between her place in life and his. A tiny pang of doubt pricked her happiness, and Jonas's words to her that morning echoed chillingly in her mind.

Her uncle and his family spoke their greetings and passed on, and Charity was left confronting the Conyngtons. She made her curtsy, but Darrell stooped to take her hands and draw her to her feet. She looked quickly up into his face, and found that he was smiling at her with all the old affection.

"Well, little one?" he said teasingly. It was his pet name for her, and merely to hear it again made her heart lift with happiness. "You are a deal more demure today than I remember you. Madam," he added, turning to his wife, "let me make known to you Charity Shenfield, of

27

whom I have told you. A troublesome brat, but we have learned to bear with her."

Alison Conyngton smiled shyly at Charity. She was a small, slender girl, exceedingly pretty, with a delicate, childish face and very dark grey eyes. Her hair was of a gold so pale that it seemed almost silvery, and in her pale, shimmering satin gown, with pearls about her throat, she seemed to Charity almost fairy-like in her daintiness. She was also exceedingly nervous, her hands clutched tightly on a folded fan, her eyes downcast save when from time to time she glanced as though for reassurance at her husband. The younger girl, herself a stranger to shyness, felt a swift rush of sympathy, tinged with impatience. It was to be the basis of her feeling for Alison all the time she knew her.

Darrell was still looking quizzically at Charity. "By my faith, child, how tall you grow!" he remarked. "Soon I shall be able to call you 'little one' no longer."

Charity laughed, for she was unperturbed by the height which, so her aunt repeatedly informed her, was most unbecoming in a woman. "Jonas says 'tis the weeds that grow the tallest."

"Jonas," Darrell said dryly, "appears to have changed but little. It is time he learned a measure of courtesy."

"Oh, he is envious, that is all," Charity replied lightly. "He would dearly love to be taller himself, and it irks him that already I lack so little of his own height. He fears that ere long I shall outstrip him altogether."

He laughed, but more guests were approaching and he had no opportunity to reply. Lady Conyngton beckoned Charity closer and drew her down to sit on a low stool beside her chair, and from a little distance away Elizabeth Shenfield frowned to see the girl so singled out. Where

28

Charity was concerned, nothing irritated Mrs Shenfield so much as the manner in which she was favoured by all the Conyngtons. The implied slight to her own children, and especially to the son of whom she was inordinately proud, was something for which she could not forgive her niece. She looked around now for Jonas, and discovered him standing alone by one of the window-embrasures, leaning against the wall and staring in a brooding fashion towards Darrell Conyngton. Her frown deepened, for it would do him no good so plainly to display the hostility he felt towards the squire's son.

Had she guessed the truth, however, she would have been even more dismayed, for it was not Darrell at whom Jonas was staring, but Darrell's bride. Until the moment when he stepped into the Long Gallery he had never even thought of Alison Conyngton, save when he had used her name that morning to taunt his cousin, but the first sight of her had taken his breath away. He had made his bow and muttered he knew not what, and then moved on in a daze, unable to think of anything but that delicately featured face, the beautiful, long-lashed eyes which for a fleeting instant had looked into his. Now he had recovered his wits a little, but still could not bring himself to join in the conversation of those about him, and could only stand and watch her, alternately cursing himself for the clumsiness which must have made him appear to her as a mannerless oaf, and Darrell because, in addition to all else, he now had this exquisite creature for his wife.

Charity, catching a glimpse of him between the shifting groups of guests, reflected that he looked even more discontented than usual, but she had little thought to spare for Jonas at that moment. She was absorbed in looking at the older people about her and in listening to their conversation, fascinating scraps of which reached her ears first from one direction and then from another. She was perfectly happy until Darrell, who had moved away to speak to someone on the other side of the room, rejoined the group around his mother's chair, and one of the gentlemen said to him:

"What news do you bring us from London, Mr Conyngton? There have been disquieting rumours of late, but it is no easy task to sift the few grains of truth from the chaff of gossip and speculation."

The question brought a momentary pause in their immediate vicinity, for all were aware that by news from London the speaker meant not trivial gossip of fashion and scandal, but words of the tension and unrest which were spreading throughout the kingdom. Charity saw Darrell's face grow suddenly grave, and it was a moment or two before he replied.

"Tidings, sir, of which I would sooner not be the bearer," he said at length. "You are aware, of course, of the impeachment and trial of Lord Strafford?" There was a little murmur of assent and he went on: "For a long while it seemed that he could not be harmed, for every charge brought against him he disproved to the satisfaction of the lawyers. It was his plea that he had broken no law, therefore he was guilty of no crime. But Pym and Hampden and their followers in the Commons sought not justice, but vengeance. When they found it impossible to convict him they passed a Bill of Attainder, and so declared him guilty by Act of Parliament."

Another murmur, this time of astonishment and dismay, made itself heard, and someone said, voicing the thoughts of them all:

"Surely the King will never give his assent?"

"His Majesty will save Lord Strafford if he can," Darrell agreed gravely, "but feeling runs high in London at present—how high you cannot realize who have not seen the terrible hostility of the populace towards his lordship. When I set out for Devon the matter hung still in the balance, but my wife's father has promised to send me word as soon as any certain news is known. When that news reaches me be sure that I shall share it with you without delay."

Charity, looking round her at the suddenly grave faces of her elders, wondered why they should be so concerned. Lord Strafford, according to Jonas, was the personification of evil, the enemy of all rights and liberties of the people—though Charity was quite prepared to believe that Jonas had either lied or was mistaken.

All around her conversation had broken out again, but where before there had been laughter and an easy exchange of pleasantries, an anxious note now sounded through the hum of talk. It was a note which persisted and spread, and died away only as the company followed Sir Darrell and his wife down the Great Hall where a sumptuous meal was laid. Then gradually a more lighthearted atmosphere began to prevail again, as though the guests had remembered that this was an occasion for rejoicing.

Charity, sitting with Beth and Jonas some distance from the table below the Minstrels' Gallery where the Conyngtons were seated with their principal guests, ate with a hearty appetite, but looked frequently towards Darrell, wondering how long it would be before she had an opportunity to talk to him again. So it happened that she was one of the few who noticed a servant bend to murmur some message in his ear, and Darrell, after a brief word with his father, rise and go quietly out of the room. He was absent for some ten minutes, and when he returned his face was pale and very grave. Once more he consulted with his father, and then Sir Darrell rose to his feet and lifted his hand for silence.

"My friends," he said as the talk and laughter died away, "I bade you here today for a joyful cause, to welcome home my son and his bride, and I little thought to dim the day's rejoicing with ill tidings. But news has just come to us from London of such grave import that I would do less than my duty if I did not acquaint you with it. Lord Strafford, God rest him, was executed three days since."

A deep, prolonged hush fell upon the company, as though with the words the cold hand of death had laid a fleeting touch upon them. Charity, though still not comprehending all the implications of what had been said, yet felt again, more strongly than before, the foreboding which had first touched her heart that morning. Then beside her Jonas laughed aloud, on a note of triumphant mockery shocking in that stricken silence. All heads turned towards him, and Sir Darrell said in a voice of stern rebuke:

"Young man, such news is no matter for mirth! Only a fool or a traitor could find cause for laughter in an event which strikes deep at everything we have been taught to revere." He paused for a moment, and then went on, addressing the whole company again: "The King used every means in his power to save his loyal servant. Even when he had given his assent to the Bill of Attainder he sent the Prince of Wales to beg the House of Lords to reduce the sentence to perpetual imprisonment, but in vain. His lordship was not even granted time to set his worldly affairs in order."

Charity was now more puzzled than ever. Why should the King need to beg? Surely he had only to command? She knew better, however, than to intrude with questions at such a time, and resolved to ask Darrell to explain it to her at the first opportunity.

Such opportunity did not occur for more than a week. At the Moat House idleness was encouraged in no one, and when lessons were done there were many domestic duties in which the three girls had to be instructed. A gentlewoman could depend upon having numerous servants, but by the time she assumed control of her own household was expected to be familiar with all their duties and capable of directing their labours. Mrs. Shenfield would have considered that she was failing in her duty if she had neglected this important part of her daughters' education, and though there seemed little likelihood that Charity would ever marry, she was being given as thorough a training as Beth and Sarah.

She applied herself to these tasks with as much diligence as she could muster, though in those bright days of early summer she would infinitely have preferred to be out of doors instead of occupied in kitchen or stillroom. Only in the early mornings before the rest of the household was awake could she enjoy any degree of freedom, and on one such morning, when she had slipped secretly from the house to roam the woods and meadows, she had the good fortune to encounter Darrell.

He was exercising one of his spirited horses, but when he caught sight of Charity waving to him he drew rein and dismounted, waiting for her to come up to him. When they had greeted each other she came to the point with her usual directness.

"I want you to explain something to me, Darrell! Why did the King allow Lord Strafford to be executed?"

He looked startled and then amused. "That is a weighty question for a fine summer morning! There is no need for *you* to plague your mind with such matters."

She scowled at him, her black brows almost meeting across the bridge of her nose. "Do not talk to me as though I were as foolish as Beth or Sarah, with no thought in my head beyond spinning or sewing or a new ribbon for my gown! I know there are grave matters afoot and I wish to understand them, but that I shall never do if no one will explain them to me."

"Peace, little one! I had forgot your unquenchable thirst for knowledge." Darrell spoke lightly, but turned to loop his horse's rein over a low-sweeping branch of a hawthorn tree which shaded a grassy bank. "Sit here with me, then, and I will strive to explain it, though, truth to tell, wiser men than I might shrink from such a task."

"On the day you came home," Charity began as soon as they were seated, " 'twas said the King was not able to save Lord Strafford's life. Is not the King the supreme power in the land?"

"The ultimate power," Darrell replied slowly, "but Parliament waxes ever stronger. In my grandfather's day, when the old Queen ruled, there was peace between Sovereign, Lords and Commons, but that peace died with her. The Stuart kings have been at odds with Parliament from the first, yet they find difficulty in ruling without it, since only through Parliament can they obtain money to maintain themselves and the Court, and to defend the realm."

Charity was silent for a space, considering this, and then said in a puzzled tone: "I know that a new Parliament was elected last year, but was that not the first for a very long time?"

"For eleven years," Darrell agreed, "for during that time the King and his advisers contrived by various means to obtain sufficient money for ordinary needs. But the war with the Scottish Covenanters created demands these could not meet, and the King was forced to summon Parliament again. It met in April of last year, and was dissolved a few weeks later."

Charity, her elbows resting on her knees, her chin on her hands, regarded him with a frown: "Why?"

Darrell shrugged. "Because the same grievances, both religious and secular, were voiced by the new Parliament as by the old, and because during the years of the King's personal rule new causes for discontent had been found."

She nodded, pleased that upon one point at least she was not entirely ignorant. "I know! Ship Money, and other unjust taxes."

He cast her a quick glance, half surprised and half amused. "Where learned you that glib talk of injustice? Not, I'll wager, from your uncle."

"From Jonas. Is it not true?"

"Many believe it, though for my part I cannot see why Ship Money should be thought so iniquitous. The Fleet defends the whole country. Why then should not all pay for its upkeep, instead of merely those counties bordering upon the sea?"

Not knowing the answer to this, Charity asked a question of her own, to bring the conversation back to its original course. "There is a Parliament now, is there not?"

"Yes, it was installed last November, for by that time the Covenanters had crossed the Border and were in possession of Durham and Northumberland, and the King's need of money could no longer be denied. Yet in the Parliamentary party many are in sympathy with the Scots and regard them as the deliverers of England. And they all hated Strafford more than any man in the land."

"But he was a very wicked man, was he not? Jonas says that he was a renegade traitor who would have brought an army of Irish papists down upon us."

"It would appear," Darrell said with a frown, "that Master Jonas says a deal which is unseemly! Where learns he such lessons in disloyalty?"

"In Plymouth, when he goes there to visit his uncles. His father knows nothing of it, nor does my aunt. Jonas would not venture to say these things to them, but, being Jonas, he must boast of his knowledge to someone. Beth and Sarah will pay no heed, and so he has no choice but to tell me. Darrell, *was* Lord Strafford so very wicked?"

Darrell pulled off his broad, plumed hat and dropped it on the grass beside him. Then he lay back against the bank, his hands clasped beneath his head, and stared up at the hawthorn blossom, white against the deep blue sky.

"He was an ambitious man, and a ruthless one," he said reflectively. "In earlier Parliaments he stood with Pym and Eliot and Coke against the King, yet during the years of the personal rule he rose to be the King's greatest and most trusted Minister. That is why the Parliamentarians named him 'traitor' and why they would not rest until he had been destroyed. But wicked? Who can say?"

Another silence fell between them, while Charity pondered all that she had been told, and Darrell lay lost in thought. It was very peaceful there at the edge of the woods. The heavy scent of the hawthorn mingled with that of the bluebells which spread their dusky carpet beneath the trees, and the sunlight reached through the branches to dapple Charity's old stuff gown and her companion's velvet doublet. Somewhere far above them a lark was singing, its voice dropping into the stillness like a thread of purest gold.

"It is good to be home!" Darrell said softly after a while. "To feel one's own land beneath one's feet, and to sleep again in the house where one was born. I believe I would gladly live out the rest of my life at Conyngton, nor set foot again beyond the borders of Devonshire."

She looked affectionately down at him, for she knew—better, perhaps, than most—his deep and passionate devotion to his fair heritage. More of his boyhood had been spent there than was usual for a lad of his rank, for Sir Darrell, having no other child, had preferred that his son be educated wholly at home instead of going in his early teens to one of the universities. All this Charity knew and to some extent could understand, for she, too, loved Conyngton. Yet to her, who had no prospect of ever journeying farther afield, the unknown world beyond beckoned constantly. Perhaps it was her father's restlessness in her, or the proud, fierce spirit of her Norman forbears, which made it difficult for her to accept with resignation her drab destiny.

"But did you then take no pleasure in this past year?" she asked wonderingly. "To go to London, to Court, to see the King and Queen—oh, Darrell, it must have given you pleasure!"

"It was well enough!" He sat upright again, shaking back his long hair. "But at Court there is intrigue and place-seeking as well as masques and dancing, and in these troublous times as much bitterness and distrust in London as amusement and gay company. Oh, I met great men and beautiful, witty women at Whitehall, and made merry with my friends in theatre and tavern, but I heard also the Puritans hurling savage abuse at the bishops and at the Church as we know it, and an armed mob howling for Strafford's head. No, little one, the best is here, where life goes on as it has always done—and where by God's grace it always will!"

The last few words were spoken softly, almost as though they were a prayer, and then for a space he was silent, his young face grave and troubled, the shadow of disquieting thoughts in his eyes. Then, becoming aware again of the girl beside him, her expression puzzled and uneasy, her intent dark gaze fixed anxiously upon his face, he deliberately cast off his heavy mood. He sprang to his feet, catching her by the hand and pulling her up with him.

"Enough of this solemnity! The sun shines, and for the present at least life is good, so let us not go seeking sorrow. Come, I will take you up behind me as far as the Moat House, for I'll warrant you should be at your lessons by now!"

"No, stay a moment!" She hung back against his grip, bringing up her other hand to grasp his wrist. "Darrell, tell me the truth! Surely these troubles in London can never touch *our* lives, here at Conyngton St John?"

He looked down at her, and she saw the shadow he had tried to banish once more darkening the hazel eyes. "They are troubles that strike deep, little one," he said slowly. "At the Church and at the State, at the King's right to rule, and the people's right to resist what some of them call tyranny. On both sides feelings run perilously high, but only God in His infinite wisdom can tell what the end will be."

3

Alison

Whenever Charity looked back upon it in after years she always thought of that as the golden summer, the last precious, carefree days of childhood before the shadows which were reaching out across the kingdom touched her life with darkness. It was a summer which brought her the promise of a happier future than she had ever dared to hope for, a promise for which she had Darrell to thank.

The first inkling of any change in her prospects came in July, just after her fourteenth birthday, when Mrs. Shenfield told her that she had been invited by Lady Conyngton to spend a week at the manor. Charity was surprised at the invitation and even more surprised that she was to be allowed to go, but accepted her good fortune without question. Delights such as this came her way all too rarely.

When she arrived at the manor, and was greeted by the two ladies, she thought that Alison looked pale, and even more subdued than she remembered from their one previous meeting, but thought little of this until the following day, when she happened to find the other girl in one of the arbours in the garden, weeping bitterly. As Charity's shadow darkened the doorway she looked up with a start and a little gasp of alarm. Charity spoke quickly to reassure her.

"Pray do not be alarmed. 'Tis I, Charity Shenfield."

"Miss Shenfield!" Alison dabbed at her eyes in a flustered way, trying to speak calmly. "Forgive me! I did not hear you approach."

"I came across the grass!" Charity moved farther into the arbour, and added in her usual, forthright way: "What is amiss?"

"Nothing! Nothing, I assure you!" Alison spoke quickly, but her quavering voice belied the words. "I am exceeding foolish. Pay no heed!" She glanced up, encountered the younger girl's direct, considering, but not unfriendly gaze, and her eyes filled again. "I am so lonely!" she added pathetically.

"Lonely? Here?" Charity sat down beside her and regarded her with astonishment. "How can that be?"

"Oh, it is wrong of me, I know! Undutiful, and ungrateful, too, when everyone is so kind, but—but I would I were not so far from my own family."

"You are a Conyngton now," Charity reminded her with some severity. "They are your family."

"Yes, and they are all so good to me, but, oh, I miss my sister so sorely! Until my marriage we had never been parted."

"I have no sisters," Charity remarked reflectively, "but I believe I would not greatly miss Beth or Sarah if I were parted from them. Perhaps, though, that is not the same."

She paused, and then added with a flash of her wide, friendly smile: "Darrell sometimes calls *me* his little sister. Would it ease your loneliness, think you, if you strove to look on me in the same fashion?"

Alison was both startled and touched. This dark, outspoken girl was like no one she had ever known, but she recognized the genuine friendliness behind the suggestion, and her spirits lifted a little in response to it. She was only sixteen, and though she had been carefully prepared for it, the prospect of shouldering the responsibilities of a great estate like Conyngton secretly terrified her. Lady Conyngton's feeble health had long obliged her to leave all the active management of the household to her cousin and waiting-gentlewoman, Miss Mary, but Miss Mary was growing old and would be glad to hand over the reins to Darrell's bride. Alison, with her mother and sisters far away, and too shy to disclose her fears to her husband or Lady Conyngton, was in desperate need of someone in whom she could confide, and grasped thankfully at Charity's proffered friendship. Hers was a gentle, compliant nature, and she sensed in the younger girl the strength of character she herself lacked.

In the days that followed, Darrell and his parents watched with satisfaction the ripening friendship between the two girls. Charity soon adopted a protective attitude towards Alison, although there were some things about her new friend she could not understand. She was astonished, even shocked, to discover that Alison was just a little afraid of her husband, for Charity's own character, and her easy, long-standing comradeship with Darrell, made such a thing inconceivable to her. She adored him, and looked up to him as she might an elder brother, but this did not prevent her from teasing him, arguing with him, even defying him on some occasions. Alison's diffidence, her instant deference to his wishes, and her breathless anxiety to please, puzzled Charity and even aroused in her a faint contempt.

Another aspect of Alison's nature which exasperated her was her timidity. Conyngton, like every great country estate, had its stables of fine horses, its hunting dogs and hawks, and for Charity the most spirited horse or fiercest dog held no terrors. She was an excellent rider, and would mount one of Darrell's own horses whenever the opportunity was offered, and he had long since initiated her into the mysteries of the chase. Alison found herself unable to share their enthusiasm. She was far happier with gentle, domestic pursuits, and only her desire to please Darrell, and the knowledge that he had gone to some trouble to procure for her a particularly docile mount, persuaded her, during Charity's visit, to ride out with them to see something of the countryside around her new home.

The first of these expeditions was entirely successful, for they rode through fertile valleys, by farm and cottage whose inhabitants were eager to give a smiling, respectful greeting to the young squire and his lady. On the second occasion, however, Darrell yielded to Charity's pleading and took the road that led northwards to Dartmoor.

Charity was fascinated by the Moor, that savage, lonely region said to be the haunt of giants and witches, where at night, so the legends told, the ghostly Yeth Hounds bayed and howled among the granite tors, urged on by demon hunters. Her imagination responded to the wildness of the Moor as it could never, love it though she did, respond to the gentle countryside around her home. The Shenfields' old nurse, from whom she had learned these eerie tales, had told her also that as a boy her father

43

had loved to ride there, and nothing pleased Charity so much as to do likewise.

As they drew near the Moor, she began to recount some of its legends to Alison. Her intentions were of the best, but she had forgotten the older girl's natural timidity, and it was left to Darrell to observe his wife's pallor, her wide, frightened eyes, and to call Charity somewhat sharply to account. Realizing the effect her tales had had, she muttered a gruff apology, and then, as though to cover her confusion, set spur to her horse and let it have its head along the rough moorland track. Alison, thinking the animal had bolted, gave a gasp of alarm, but Darrell smiled and shook his head.

"Be easy, my dear, she will come to no harm," he said lightly. "Think you I would have mounted her on yon brute had I not been certain that she can manage it?" He gave her a searching glance. "She frightened you, did she not, with her tales of ghosts and goblins?"

She looked about her and shivered. They had set out from Conyngton in bright sunshine, but though the lower country behind them was still bathed in sunlight, they had ridden into gathering cloud and the Moor lay wild and menacing under a threatening sky.

"She meant no harm, I know," she replied in a low voice, "but this place makes me fearful. How *can* Charity like to come here?" She looked timidly at him. "Forgive me, if you can, for such folly! I would I had but one small part of her hardihood!"

Darrell laughed, turning upon her a glance both tender and amused. Their marriage, after the custom of the day, had been a matter of arrangement between his father and hers, but he counted himself exceptionally fortunate in his bride. He was proud of her beauty, while her gentle, timid nature aroused all that was chivalrous in his own, so that to cherish and protect her seemed the most natural thing in the world. The wistfulness in her last words did not escape him, and he leaned across to take her hand and lift it briefly to his lips.

"You are very well as you are," he assured her gently, "and never think that I would have you otherwise. Charity is a valiant little soul, but a wild piece, a madcap who would have been better born a lad than a maid."

"I believe she wishes herself that it had been so!" Alison had flushed with pleasure at his words, and now lifted her eyes worshipfully to his. "She has already come to mean much to me, but I will own that in some ways she is beyond my comprehension. She is a strange, restless child, is she not, as unlike her cousins in nature as in looks?"

"Hers is a strange and restless history," he replied, "and I have heard that in character her father bore scant resemblance to his sober brother. Robert Shenfield was a wild blade, from all accounts, and when little more than a lad became involved in a scandal which made his departure from this neighbourhood a matter of some urgency. Thereafter his family heard naught of him for seven years, at the end of which time came a letter to say that he had married a French wife."

"A papist?" Alison's voice was shocked, for though the Queen of England was both a Frenchwoman and a Catholic, she, and those who shared her faith, were regarded by many with abhorrence and distrust.

Darrell shook his head. "No, the lady came of a Huguenot family, but even so the match did not commend itself to Jonathan Shenfield, especially since the marriage had been forbidden by her father, and Robert carried her

45

off in spite of him, so that she came to him dowerless."
He laughed softly. "Perhaps 'carried her off' is not the
best choice of phrase, since it implies a measure of un-
willingness on her part. My mother will tell you—and she
had it from Marguerite Shenfield herself—that she escaped from her father's house disguised in her page's
clothes, and travelled thus all the way to England. Can
you marvel that the union of two so reckless natures
should have produced such a daughter as Charity?"

Alison still looked faintly shocked, for nothing in her
decorous and ordered upbringing had prepared her for
revelations such as these. After a moment or two, however, compassion outweighed decorum, and she said:

"No, indeed, and she is doubly to be pitied in being left
an orphan. Did she never know her parents?"

Darrell shook his head, his gaze following Charity's flying figure, now small with distance. "No, poor brat, for
Robert Shenfield was killed in a tavern brawl in London
within a year of his marriage. When the news reached his
family his brother travelled thither and found the widow
near destitute. He brought her back to the Moat House,
where she died when Charity was born a few months
later. I cannot recall her, but my mother came to know
her well and to have a deep regard for her."

"Charity means a great deal to Lady Conyngton," Alison remarked, adding, after an instant's hesitation: "And
to you also, does she not?"

"Yes, she does," he replied promptly. "I could not
have a greater fondness for her were she in truth my sister. I am glad that you and she have become friends, for
it troubles me sometimes to think what the future may
hold for her. With two daughters of his own, it is not
likely that Mr Shenfield will dower her, and if she does

46

not wed it will go hard with her after his death. Her cousin Jonas has no liking for her. It is in my mind that we should make her future our concern." He paused for a moment, and then went on, watching her closely to see the effect of his words: "You have need of a companion, a waiting-gentlewoman. What say you to Charity in that office?"

Alison's eyes lit with pleasure. She would have been willing to agree to the suggestion merely to please him, but she could in all honesty say that it would please her also. Already she had come to depend on Charity to an extent she had scarcely realized until now.

"There is nothing I would like better," she replied eagerly, "but will her uncle consent?"

"I believe so. To be frank with you, he knows that that was the thought behind Charity's present visit to us, but I wished you both to become acquainted with each other before any decision was reached." He paused, for Charity had turned her horse and was galloping back towards them. Darrell looked humorously at his wife. "Say naught to her yet. She is already in a mad enough humour this day."

Charity reined in beside them with a flourish. Her eyes were sparkling and her whole face in a glow, so that for a moment she looked almost handsome.

"That was splendid!" she exclaimed, leaning forward to pat her mount's glossy neck. "If only I might always ride such a horse! But we have only one or two in our stables to match with yours, and those we have, *I* am not permitted to ride."

Darrell grinned at her. "You cannot expect your uncle or Jonas to let a wild slip of a girl ride their horses. They are not as besotted as I."

"Jonas?" Charity gave a derisive chuckle. "*His* horses have as much spirit as a yoke of oxen! I would sooner mount my own old pony, whose docility is due to nothing more than age."

"Charity, your hair is coming down again!" Alison, always impeccably neat herself, regarded her young friend despairingly. "Can you do nothing to keep it tidy?"

"No, for 'tis too heavy for pins or ribbons to hold in place," Charity replied unconcernedly, pushing back the black tresses. "I've a mind to cut it off, and have it loose on my shoulders as Darrell wears his." She chuckled again as Alison, rising to the bait, uttered a shocked protest, and then, her thoughts taking a fresh direction, continued blithely: "I believe I have not told you of Jonas's newest freak! He came home from Plymouth last week with his long curls cropped off, saying that lovelocks are a vanity of the devil. My poor aunt wept bitterly at sight of him."

"As well she might!" Darrell's voice was suddenly grim. "Mr Shenfield would do well to forbid Jonas's visits to his uncles in Plymouth. It seems they are turning him into a curst Puritan."

"Perhaps he will," she replied cheerfully. "He was mightily displeased, and said he would go to Plymouth himself to see them. When I left the Moat House Jonas was sulking, and his mother still lamenting the loss of his golden curls. Oh, 'twas a merry household, I give you my word!"

"This is something I cannot understand!" Darrell said angrily. "Jonas has been reared in traditions of loyalty, taught a proper reverence for the Church and for the King. What then draws him to these fanatical beliefs?"

Charity, riding beside him as they began to retrace

their steps, looked mischievously up at him. "The desire to find favour in his uncles' eyes," she replied shrewdly, "and the sheer preversity of his nature. Surely you know, Darrell, that Jonas must ever hold views which are the exact opposite of yours?"

He frowned. "If you are right, then 'tis the worst reason in the world for so betraying the beliefs in which he had been reared. If sincere conviction drew him to the Puritan faith I might detest him for it, but at least I could respect him. Hypocrisy can only bring down upon him the contempt of all honest men."

When the end of Charity's stay at the manor drew near, Lady Conyngton told her of the tentative plans made for her future. The girl could find no words to reply, but she dropped to one knee and caught her ladyship's frail hand to her lips, and the gesture, and the happiness and gratitude shining in her eyes, spoke more clearly than any speech. Later, finding herself alone with Darrell, she said earnestly:

"Her ladyship has told me, Darrell, that it was *your* thought to bring me here as waiting-gentlewoman to your wife. There can be no need for me to tell you how grateful I am."

"Nor need for gratitude, either, little one," he replied affectionately. "I am happy to know that the future well-being of my little sister is to be my concern."

"You will not regret it," she promised in a low voice, and with unwonted gravity. "If my uncle consents to my coming I will spend the rest of my life striving to be worthy of the trust you put in me."

Mr Shenfield did consent, with only one reservation. Charity, he said, was too young as yet for such responsibility, but as soon as she reached her fifteenth birthday, if

Mrs Conyngton still desired it, she should go to live at the manor. Meanwhile, she might continue to visit Conyngton as often as her presence there was required. Charity was disappointed, but, thankful that permission had not been withheld altogether, resolved to be patient, and to prove, by her conduct during the next twelve months, that she had put the follies of childhood behind her for ever.

Beth and Sarah accepted her proposed departure from the Moat House with indifference, but Jonas received the news with a curious mixture of anger, jealousy, and contempt. Jonas, however, grew more intractable each day. Although his father had made the threatened visit to Plymouth, it soon became evident that this had resulted neither in any curtailment of his son's freedom nor in a quarrel with Mrs Shenfield's brothers. At intervals during the summer one or both of them would visit the Moat House, and though there was nothing remarkable in this— such visits had taken place ever since Charity could remember—she realized now that a subtle change had gradually come about in the two merchants.

They had always been grave men, soberly dressed and somewhat slow to mirth, but now their clothes were aggressively sombre, their hair cropped short, and their conversation liberally sprinkled with Biblical texts and quotations from the Scriptures. They frowned upon the gay silk gowns their sister and her daughters and niece wore in honour of their visits, and on one occasion the elder of the two, finding the three girls amusing themselves with dancing and singing, rebuked them with a severity which reduced Beth and Sarah to tears, and Charity to furious, smouldering-eyed resentment. These, then, were the Puritans of whom Darrell had told her, the fanatics who had yelled for Strafford's life, who defied the King and reviled his beloved Queen, and condemned the beautiful, stately Court at Whitehall as a place of extravagance and vice. She watched and listened to them, and encouraged Jonas to go on confiding in her, and all the while her revulsion grew and with it fear of the threat to peace and happiness which they and their kind embodied.

Yet in those months following Lord Strafford's execution the tide of popular feeling seemed to turn in favour of the King. With the "wicked Earl" dead, Archbishop Laud in the Tower, and the rest of Charles's hated advisers fled overseas, many people in England began to turn against the fanatical Puritan party which had previously seemed the champion of liberty against Royal oppression. The Puritans' war upon the Established Church, their dealings with the Scottish invaders, most of all, perhaps, their constant, savage attacks on all worldly pleasures, however innocent, aroused bitter antagonism among more moderate people. Many changes had been made, many tyrannies removed. Surely the kingdom could now rest content?

The months moved slowly past, midsummer revels gave way to the harvest home, and summer began to yield place to autumn. At Conyngton and the Moat House, and in the little village of Conyngton St John, the seasons followed their accustomed course, seemingly undisturbed by the fierce dissensions smouldering elsewhere, yet even in that sleepy backwater conflict was already making itself felt. The Conyngtons themselves were fiercely Royalist, and the majority of the neighbours and tenants followed their example, but there were one or two who, like Jonas Shenfield, tended towards the other point of view.

Charity herself had no doubt at all where her own loyalty lay. Just as all her affection was given to Darrell Conyngton and his family, so their faith was hers, their beliefs and devotion echoed in her own heart. As the months passed she drew ever closer to them, and farther away from her own kin. She spent more and more time at the manor, performing small services for Lady Conyngton, bearing Alison company in a score of diverse domestic tasks, learning from Darrell all she could of the differences which were splitting the country from end to end.

Her appetite for knowledge was insatiable, her interest in these events exceeding by far that of Alison or Lady Conyngton. Her ladyship's precarious health bound the whole household in an unspoken conspiracy to keep from her the true gravity of the situation, while for Alison the small pleasures and duties of every day were of more importance than the failure of the King to establish a reconciliation with the Scots, or the unspeakable horrors of cruelty and violence which that autumn broke forth in Ireland, hitherto kept at peace by Strafford's strong hand. Alison was happy now at Conyngton. She no longer fretted for her mother and sisters, and the only cloud upon her contentment was that her longing for a child was as yet unfulfilled.

Christmas came, and according to custom the hospitable doors of Conyngton were opened to gentle and simple alike. Charity loved the Christmas revels at Conyngton, the music and dancing, the mummers with their plays, the festive dishes and the general atmosphere of gaiety and affection which seemed to enfold everybody in one great, joyful embrace. The times might be troubled, the whole land plagued by dissensions growing too bitter to be resolved by words alone, but everyone at

Conyngton, from Sir Darrell himself to the humblest serving-maid, seemed determined that for the twelve days of Christmas all care and anxiety should be set aside.

Jonas did not accompany his family to the manor. He had taken to wearing sober colours and plain linen, after the fashion affected by his two uncles, and when told that they were all bidden, as usual, to share the Christmas festivities at Conyngton, refused point-blank to go with them. Instead he saddled his horse and rode off to Plymouth, to spend the time, he said, in a seemly manner unmarred by any heathen revelry.

Yes, Jonas had changed, Charity reflected as she stood in one of the window-embrasures of the Long Gallery, watching the merry scene before her, and she felt sorry for the girl in the northern part of the county whom Mr Shenfield was seeking as a bride for his son. The negotiations had been begun in the summer, and still showed no sign of reaching a successful conclusion. Beth's future had been more easily settled. She was already betrothed, and would be married in the spring. There were many changes imminent at the Moat House.

"Why so thoughtful, little one?" Darrell had come unobserved to join her, and now stood leaning one hand against the wall and looking quizzically down at her. " 'Tis unlike you to be so solemn."

"I was thinking of Jonas," Charity replied candidly, "and that I do not envy the young lady he is to marry. It is to be hoped that she does not lack spirit, for, by my faith, she will have need of it!"

"Yes, in her place you would lead him a merry dance, would you not?" Darrell's tone was amused, his glance affectionate as it rested upon her face. He was glad that the question of her coming to live at the manor was satisfactorily settled, for he disliked Jonas Shenfield in his new Puritan guise even more than he had done hitherto. Jonas was old enough now for his word to begin to carry some weight, and his father might be swayed by his opinions, which would certainly not favour anything which gave satisfaction to Charity or to the Conyngtons.

"Ah well!" Charity had been following her own train of thought. "Perhaps it may all come to naught after all. I hear that the lady's father seems not over-eager for the match."

"He might be more so if Jonas paid less heed to his uncles' teaching," Darrell replied dryly. "What loyal gentleman, as I believe him to be, desires a crop-headed, psalm-singing Puritan for his daughter's husband? Your uncle, Charity, would have been well advised to check that folly at the outset."

"Mayhap he does not altogether count it folly," Charity retorted wisely. "The two worthy merchants have long purses and no other heir. Oh, plague take Jonas, and his uncles, too! Let us go join the dance!"

4

The Shadow Darkens

It was a cold, bleak afternoon towards the middle of January. A bitter north-east wind scourged the countryside, and the clouds hung low and grey, big with the threat of snow. At the Moat House the family gathered close about the great fireplace in the big, stone-flagged, oak-panelled hall which was still the principal room of the house. It was an uncomfortable apartment, separated from the main entrance only by massive screens of carved wood, and with the staircase rising at its farther end. Draughts whistled through it, although the windows were set above the height of a man's head and a fire of huge logs blazed fiercely on the hearth. Charity, surreptitiously tucking her skirts closer about her chilled ankles, reflected that they would all have been far more comfortable in the parlour which was her aunt's special domain, but Jonathan Shenfield was a man who disliked change, and preferred to sit, as his forbears had sat in more rugged days, in the largest and most imposing room in the house.

He sat now in his large, high-backed chair, a branch of candles on a small table beside him enabling him to read aloud to his family from the book of sermons which rested on his knee. Mrs Shenfield and the three girls were busy with their needles, but Jonas sat idle, his feet outstretched towards the fire and a frown wrinkling his brow. He looked sullen and angry, and now and then his mother cast him an anxious glance. She feared that his black looks were caused by the sermon his father was reading, for it was the product of a noted Anglican divine and Jonas now made no secret of his Puritan beliefs. These had not yet led to an open rift with his father, but there had been much bickering and she feared another outbreak of it now.

Had she but known it, however, her son's thoughts were so far removed from the sermon that he scarcely heard a word of it. Jonas was, in fact, exceedingly troubled and perplexed, for many stormy emotions were seething within him and seemed to be dragging him in several different directions at once.

In the beginning his conversion to the Puritan faith had been affected merely to curry favour with his uncles, but he had since been influenced by the arguments and opinions he had heard expressed in their houses. These stated absolutely that it was the duty of every right-thinking Englishman to do his utmost to root out privilege and the tyranny of the King, to destroy the bishops and free the Church from all threat of Catholic domination. The Puritan preachers, obsessed by the savagery of the Old Testament, by their own fierce God of wrath and terrible

56

vengeance, had struck a ready response from some hitherto unsuspected quality in Jonas's nature.

Yet for all his new Puritan zeal, there was another side of his character, the practical, almost avaricious streak which had prompted him in the first place to adopt the beliefs of his rich, childless uncles in order to remain in their favour. This had by no means been defeated, and just as he had learned to dress and act in what the two merchants considered a seemly manner, so he was reluctant to risk a real breach with his father. It was a time when many families were beginning to be divided by opposing loyalties, and Jonas sometimes feared that in his endeavours to secure his uncles' fortune he risked losing his patrimony. Jonathan Shenfield lacked the passionate, unswerving loyalty of the Conyngtons, but he was far from sharing the views of the more violent opponents of the King, and with his inherent dislike of change seemed more likely to support the monarchy and the Established Church than to oppose them. Jonas sought a middle course, which would endanger none of his expectations yet still place no undue burden upon his conscience.

That conscience already bore a sufficiently heavy load, for Jonas, in addition to his other problems, was still suffering from the thwarted pangs of first love. From the moment of setting eyes on Alison Conyngton he had been unable to put her out of his mind, and the fact that she was scarcely aware of his existence served only to increase his infatuation. He knew that she adored her husband and was blissfully happy in her marriage, and his old, childish jealousy of Darrell was deepened by that knowledge into something very close to hatred. Nor was his mental conflict eased by the faith he had adopted, for the Puritan preoccupation with sin and damnation reminded him constantly of the peril to his immortal soul which he courted in thus breaking the tenth Commandment. His was a state of mind potentially explosive, potentially dangerous.

Mr Shenfield came to the end of the sermon, and in the pause which followed there sounded through the winter dusk, above the moaning of the wind, the beat of rapidly approaching hoof-beats. The group around the fire looked at one another in surprise, for this was neither the hour nor the season at which a chance visitor might be expected.

An abrupt summons sounded upon the main door, a servant went to answer it, and after a few moments Darrell came through the screens into the hall. There was a light powdering of snow on his heavy cloak, in his wind-tossed hair, and on the plumed hat which he swept off as he bowed to Mrs Shenfield, and his face looked pale and grim.

"Darrell!" Mr Shenfield rose to his feet and went forward to greet him. "What do you here on so inclement a day? Is aught amiss at Conyngton?"

Darrell shook his head. "No more at Conyngton, sir, than at any other house in the kingdom," he replied gravely. "We have just received news from the Court, and my father deemed it best to inform our neighbours of it without delay. He has sent messengers to every house of note within ten miles, but to you I wished to bring the tidings myself."

As he spoke he had followed Mr Shenfield closer to the fire, pulling off his gloves and stretching out his hands to the blaze. Jonas had risen and now stood behind his chair, gripping its back, his gaze fixed on the newcomer with a curious intensity of expression.

58

Charity, too, was looking at Darrell, knowing beyond all doubt that the news he brought was bad. He had scarcely glanced at her, and that without a smile and she needed nothing more to realize how deeply he was troubled. Her aunt was fussing around him, urging him to be seated, to take off his cloak, to let her send for some refreshment, and Charity felt like screaming at her to be silent, so that Darrell might tell them what had brought him to the Moat House through the gathering darkness of a winter nightfall. She was thankful when Jonathan Shenfield himself interposed.

"Madam, there is news to be told, and I fancy the telling of it will brook no delay," he said firmly, and turned to the visitor. "Well, Darrell?"

"Not well, Mr Shenfield, but ill," Darrell replied grimly. "As ill a piece of news as we are ever like to hear. The King and Queen, and all the Court, have been forced to leave London, driven out by rioting, rebellious mobs, while the City defies its Sovereign and refuses to render up to him the enemies who have sought refuge within its boundaries."

"Merciful God!" Mr Shenfield sank down again into his chair, staring at Darrell as though he could not believe the evidence of his ears. "But why? What provoked such a storm?"

"It seems, sir, that His Majesty wearied at last of the insolence of the Commons, and resolved to impeach five of the ring-leaders—Pym and Hampden and three others—for treason. Their traitorous dealings with the Scots during the late war was warrant enough, all else aside. It was his purpose to go in person to arrest them, but somehow the intention was betrayed, and by the time the King and his gentlemen reached the House, those he sought had fled by way of the river and taken refuge in the City."

"And the City refuses to give them up!" It was Jonas who spoke, his voice unsteady and eager. "Ah, that was bravely done! God be praised for delivering them from peril!"

"Say 'the devil be praised' and you will come nearer the truth," Darrell retorted bitterly. "They are rebels and traitors every one, and the magistrates and train-bands of the City who protect them no better than they!" He turned to Mr Shenfield. "It is an ill day, sir, which sees the enemies of the King spoken of with admiration beneath your roof."

Mr Shenfield looked harrassed. He was a peaceable man, not greatly concerned with events beyond the immediate boundaries of his own small and hitherto secure world, and asked little of life save that it should continue as it had always done. He had little sympathy with the Conyngtons' passionate devotion to the Royal cause, and even less with his own son's newly acquired Puritan zeal. The two young men, confronting each other so angrily in the shadowy, candlelit room, seemed to him suddenly to personify the two opposing factions which were in the process of tearing England asunder, and he strove ineffectively to keep the peace between them, knowing even as he did so that peace was slipping from his grasp for ever.

"It is an ill day, Darrell, which sees bad feeling between my family and yours. Let us have done with it, in God's name! Tempers may run high in London, but that, surely, is no cause to endanger a friendship which has endured for generations."

"You are mistaken, sir!" Darrell's voice was cold. "The time is coming when every man will need to choose which road to follow, whether of loyalty or of rebellion, and no considerations of friendship or even of the ties of blood can be permitted to stand in the way. I believe Jonas will agree with me on that, though we can agree on nothing else."

"Aye," Jonas replied promptly. "London has shown the way and soon all England will follow. Privilege will be swept away, and with it the abuses which have brought this country to the verge of ruin. The canker of papistry shall be burned out and all men be free to worship God according to their conscience. Parliament will save not only England but the whole Protestant faith!"

"There speaks the rebel, the canting Puritan!" Darrell said contemptuously. "Are you a rogue, Jonas, or merely a fool? Do you truly believe that your insolent rabble and the mob that bays at its command can prevail against an anointed King and all those who will rally to his support?"

For a second or two Jonas stood regarding him. His face was pale with excitement, his eyes fairly blazing. All the fervour he felt for the Puritan faith, all his personal animosity towards Darrell, throbbed in his voice as he flung back a triumphant reply.

"Do you believe that they will not? It is not Parliament that has fled in disorder from London. 'Tis the Royal tyrant, and the popish whore he fetched from France to be our Queen!"

They all heard Darrell's hard, swift intake of breath, and then before anyone could move he stepped forward and struck Jonas across the face, so hard that he staggered and, losing his balance on the worn flagstones, fell sprawling across a big carved chest against the wall. Mrs Shenfield screamed, and her husband started forward to interpose his own solid person between the two younger men.

"Be easy, Mr Shenfield!" Darrell drew back and spoke

very calmly, though his face was white and a cold fury sounded in his voice. "There will be no vulgar brawling. I have abused your hospitality and I ask your pardon, but no man alive speaks thus of Their Majesties in my hearing." He looked at Jonas, who had dragged himself upright and was dabbing in a disbelieving way at the blood trickling from his lower lip. "You shall have satisfaction for that blow, Jonas, when and where you will."

He picked up his hat and gloves from the stool where he had placed them, bowed punctiliously to Mrs Shenfield and the girls, and then turned and walked briskly towards the screens masking the door. Against the stone floor his spurred boots sounded with a faint, martial music, and one hand rested on the hilt of his sword, thrusting the scabbard up beneath the heavy folds of the cloak. In silence they watched him go, stunned by the news he had brought, and by the sudden eruption of violence which had shattered their peace and quietude and which seemed but the herald of greater violence to come. The heavy door of the house had closed behind him before Charity awoke from her stupor of dismay and sprang in pursuit, paying no heed to her uncle's querulous command to her to say where she was.

Darting through the screens, she dragged the door open again and ran out into the gathering darkness. The wind struck her with an icy force which for an instant deprived her of breath, and a flurry of frozen snowflakes stung her face. Darrell was walking quickly in the direction of the stables, but he halted when he heard her call his name, and turned towards her. She ran to him and clutched him by the arm.

"What does this news really mean?" she asked in a low, urgent voice. "Darrell, tell me!"

"It means war," he replied grimly. "War of the bitterest and most bloody kind, not against a foe from another land but against each other. Nothing can stop it now! It is coming as surely as at this moment night is drawing in upon us."

Charity shivered, for it seemed to her that the words held a fearful, prophetic warning. Night was indeed drawing in, a night of bitter hatreds, of violence and suffering and the destruction of all that was bright and familiar and dear. Who could tell when the dawn would come again, or what it would reveal? As she stood there in the wintry dusk, under the darkening, leaden sky, it was as though for an instant she could see beyond all the high passions and the burning conviction of right with which each opposing faction armoured itself to the desolation the conflict must bring, and though she could only dimly comprehend what she saw, it filled her with a sense of helpless dread. She gave an incoherent exclamation and buried her face against Darrell's sleeve.

"Little one, have I frightened you?" His voice was immediately contrite. "I spoke without thought, and still in the anger which Jonas provoked. There *will* be war, for the King's enemies must be vanquished if we are ever to know peace again, but who can doubt that right will speedily prevail? Come, lift your head! My valiant little comrade must not fail me at the very outset!"

Obedient to the rallying tone of those latter words she looked up at him, forcing a smile. It was too dark for him clearly to see her face, and her voice was firm enough as she spoke for the first time a lie which was to be more than once upon her lips in the years to come.

"I am not afraid!" She squared her shoulders, trying to

subdue her trembling. " 'Tis but the cold that made me shiver."

"Aye, what am I thinking of? You are like to take a chill in this bitter wind." He put her arm round her, and with it a fold of the thick cloak, holding her close beside him. "Come, I will take you in."

"Not that way!" Charity hung back as he started towards the main door. "I will walk with you to the stableyard, and go in through the kitchens."

"As you please." Darrell turned again towards the stables and for a few yards they walked in silence. Then Charity said abruptly:

"I am glad you struck Jonas! I would have liked to hit him myself for speaking so of the King and Queen."

"Charity!" Darrell's voice was troubled. "Does your uncle share his son's sentiments to any degree? Is he for the King or for Parliament?"

"I know not!" she replied frankly. "Sometimes I think he is neither—or perhaps both. 'Tis as though he were being urged in two different directions at once, and wishes to go neither way."

"I fear there are many like him," Darrell said with a sigh, "but, soon or late, the choice will have to be made. This is a conflict from which no man can stand aloof."

They parted in the stableyard, and Darrell fetched his horse and rode home in deep and troubled thought. Arriving at Conyngton, he went straight to his father and told him everything that had happened at the Moat House. Sir Darrell listened with grave attention.

"Jonas has no choice but to demand satisfaction," he said when the tale had been told. "He will have no stomach for the fight, but he *must* meet you or be for ever dishonoured. He is but an indifferent swordsman. You may kill him or spare him, as you see fit." He paused, and looked inquiringly at his son.

"If I kill him 'twill be one traitor the less," Darrell said sombrely. "I would gladly have struck him dead today as he stood spitting out his venom against the King and Queen, and yet . . ."

"Yet you hesitate, and I think I can guess the cause," his father concluded quietly. " 'Tis Charity, is it not?"

Darrell nodded, the trouble deepening in his eyes. "If Jonas dies at my hands there will be no question of her coming to live in this house. It might even be that her uncle and aunt would bear her a grudge on my account, knowing of the affection between us, and treat her harshly because of it. Have I the right to place that burden upon her?"

Sir Darrell shook his head. "My son, I cannot tell you that. No man can. The decision must be yours alone." He got up from his chair and came to lay his hand briefly on the young man's shoulder. "Pray for guidance, that it may be granted to you to choose aright."

Three days later Darrell Conyngton and Jonas Shenfield met to settle their differences with cold steel. Their rendezvous was the bowling-green behind the Conyngton Arms, the ground iron-hard, the cropped turf crisp and frosty beneath their feet, and Jonas came to it in mortal dread. He would have killed his opponent without a qualm had it lain in his power to do so, and had no doubt that Darrell's sentiments were the same as his own. He had fetched two of his friends from Plymouth to act as his seconds, for word of the quarrel and its cause had leaked out, and, knowing the Royalist temper of the countryside, he had thought it unlikely that any there would support him.

It was not unusual for the seconds as well as the principals to fight, but on this occasion Darrell, advised by his father, was determined to prevent this if he could. The issues involved were so great, and popular feeling now running so high, that it would be fatally easy to spark off a pitched battle. When all were assembled he spoke, briefly and to the point.

"Gentlemen, we are all likely to have our fill of fighting in the months to come, and whichever cause conscience leads us to espouse we shall not serve it by needlessly squandering lives today. This quarrel is a personal one between Mr Shenfield and myself. Let it therefore be resolved by us alone."

With some reluctance this was agreed upon, and Jonas, convinced that his last hour had come, found himself engaging his adversary alone. Now even hatred was swallowed up by fear. Fear of death, fear of pain, possessing and blinding him so that his defence was clumsy and mechanical, an instinctive response to the weight of the sword in his hand, the menace of the bright blade confronting him. So certain was he of impending death that he could almost feel the cruel steel tearing through flesh and sinew, and it was with nothing but astonishment that he felt instead his weapon turned effortlessly aside and its hilt grasped in Darrell's left hand, while the point of Darrell's own sword gleamed before his eyes.

"The Disarm!" Darrell said coldly, and took the weapon from his adversary's suddenly slackened grip.

Jonas stood staring at him, his arms hanging limply at his sides; he was unable at first to realize that death had, after all, passed him by. Darrell handed his own sword to one of his seconds and took Jonas's into his right hand. On three sides the bowling-green was bordered by thick, high hedges, and on the fourth by the river which now ran black and swift and fringed with ice. For a moment Darrell stood, balancing the captured sword in his hand, and then he swung his arm and the weapon sailed in an arc through the frosty air and splashed into the hurrying water.

"Yonder is one sword at least which shall never be raised against the King," he said in the same cold voice, and then turned his back on Jonas and walked quickly towards the inn.

Jonas stood staring after him, his face livid with fury. He felt no gratitude for the mercy shown him, only anger at his swift and ignominious defeat, the humiliation which had been publicly put upon him. In that instant his hatred of Darrell Conyngton became implacable, a driving force which was to govern his life and not rest until the uttermost repayment had been exacted.

The final seal was set upon his humiliation by the fact that the duel and its outcome soon became common knowledge. Jonas had never been greatly liked, and in that staunchly Royalist community his conversion to Puritan beliefs had lately aroused deep resentment. News of his defeat was seized upon with glee and recounted time and again, losing nothing in the telling, so that within twenty-four hours Jonas had reached the conclusion that life in Conyngton St John would in future be intolerable. He resolved to take himself and his injured pride to Plymouth, where he was sure of a welcome from his uncles, and where, through them, he could achieve the consequence he craved.

His announcement of this intention provoked a storm of protest from his mother, but, scold and weep as she might, she could neither persuade her son to change his mind nor her husband to forbid his departure. Mr Shenfield had an uneasy suspicion that such a command would not be obeyed, and preferred not to put it to the test. He was, moreover, deeply sensible of the sorry figure his son had made in the recent duel, and though profoundly thankful that Darrell had spared his life, wanted no further trouble between the two young men.

So Jonas, making his preparations to depart, was not put to the necessity of deliberately disobeying his father. When all was ready, and the family assembled in the hall to bid him farewell, Charity was found to be missing. She had gone, old Nurse informed them, to carry a basket of comforts to one of the cottagers whose children were ill. Mrs Shenfield, who was weeping as much at the cause of her son's departure as at the fact of his going, said bitterly through her tears:

"Can she not even do her cousin the courtesy of bidding him farewell, the mannerless, ungrateful baggage? She has too great a conceit of herself."

"Calm yourself, madam! I care nothing for her absence," Jonas replied scornfully. "There is not so great a degree of affection between us that I yearn for a last glimpse of her."

"This is deliberately to insult you," his mother said fretfully, "and she shall be punished for it, I promise you that." Her tears welled up again and she flung her arms about him. "Oh, my son, I beg you not to go!"

"Peace, woman! The boy goes but to Plymouth," Mr Shenfield broke in testily. "And had he learned to curb his tongue he could have bided peacefully at home." He raised his hand to check the impassioned retort which was obviously on his son's lips. "No, Jonas, I will hear no more! Whether you be right or wrong I know not, but of one thing I am certain. Since you cannot back your words with deeds, you will be safer in Plymouth than here in Conyngton St John."

With an effort Jonas choked back what he had been about to say, and instead took leave of his mother and sisters. He parted from his father stiffly and without warmth, and as he rode away from the house the elder man's words lingered unpleasantly in his memory. He was, in fact, in a thoroughly unpleasant mood, which was not soothed by the prospect of a ride of some miles through the snow which, after threatening for days, had that morning begun to fall steadily. An encounter with Charity just before he reached the gateway dividing the park from the lane scattered the last shreds of his temper.

She was dressed in a hooded cloak of scarlet cloth such as the countrywomen wore, and mounted on her old grey pony which plodded slowly through the deepening snow. Jonas reined in his horse as he came abreast of her, the mounted servant behind him halting also, and addressed her with savage irony.

"Well met, cousin! I am touched to find you coming home in such haste to bid me god-speed."

Charity looked at him, her dark eyes sparkling with mischief. Snowflakes were clinging to her black hair, and to the brilliantly coloured cloak which became her so well.

"Why, coz, how could I guess the need for haste? Methought that before leaving the village you would be obliged to go a-fishing, but I see I was mistaken." Her glance went mockingly to the sword that hung at his side. "How prudent of you to have more than one."

The manservant was betrayed into a snigger which he turned hurriedly into a cough. Jonas swung round in the saddle to glare at him.

"Ride on, sirrah! I will deal with you presently." He waited until the command had been obeyed and then turned again to Charity. "You have a shrewish tongue, my girl! Beware lest it lead you into trouble."

She flung back her head and laughed aloud, the sound of her mirth ringing out across the snow-clad park to bring another smile to the lips of the departing servant. "Doth the devil rebuke sin now, Jonas? 'Tis not *my* tongue has provoked most trouble of late. Yours could have wrought your death had Darrell not shown you mercy."

Jonas's face, already pale with anger, went whiter yet, and his lips twisted venomously. All the humiliation of that moment by the river, all his overmastering jealousy and hatred of Darrell Conyngton, swept over him with renewed force. He leaned from the saddle to grasp the pony's bridle, and spoke in a low fierce voice with his face only a few inches from Charity's.

"It is a mercy he will live to regret. I tell you, cousin, a day will come when he shall wish with all his heart that he had slain me while it was in his power to do so. I do not forget, nor will I be content until I see his damned Conyngton pride humbled and trodden into the dust. Before God I swear it!"

He let her mount go, and spurred his own forward in pursuit of the servant, and Charity turned to watch him until he had passed through the gateway and out of sight. Then she urged the pony on again across the grey and silent park, through the falling snow.

"So cries the popinjay," she said aloud. "Great voice and empty words!" But though she spoke scornfully, the laughter had faded from her eyes and there was a little chill of foreboding upon her heart.

5

For Church and King

In the months that followed, Charity succeeded, if not in forgetting Jonas's threats, at least in convincing herself that they had been mere bravado. Jonas did not return to the Moat House, even for his sister's marriage in April, nor did his parents visit him, though his mother sent him regular and loving messages. The temper of Plymouth was different from that of the surrounding countryside. The seamen who frequented the town, the rich merchants who dwelt there, upheld the claims of Parliament, and the division was becoming ever more strongly marked between them and the people of the predominantly Royalist country parishes.

It was plain that Jonas Shenfield had thrown in his lot irrevocably with those who opposed the King, and in Conyngton St John folk looked askance upon his family, wondering if their sympathies lay in the same direction. Nor were these doubts confined to the immediate vicinity of the Moat House. The gentleman in North Devon whose daughter Jonathan Shenfield had sought for his son's bride broke off the arrangements, stating flatly that he would have no rebel in his family.

Although negotiations between King and Parliament continued throughout the spring and early summer of 1642, everyone knew that civil war was now inevitable. London was wholly lost to the King, who after his withdrawal had moved by stages to the north and was now in York, while the Queen had fled to Holland upon the pretext of taking their daughter, ten-year-old Princess Mary, to her chosen husband, the Prince of Orange. No one doubted that she had in fact gone to raise arms and money, and to recruit trained officers. Peace had reigned in England for many years, and save for a few gentlemen who had seen service in foreign wars, everyone was ignorant of military matters.

Between the Moat House and Conyngton a kind of formal civility had replaced the easy friendship of happier days, and only Charity maintained any close connection with Sir Darrell's family. She waited impatiently for the time when she would go to live at the manor, for she was fearful always that something would occur to prevent it, and meanwhile she spent as much time there as was permissible. Her fears proved groundless. July saw her enter her sixteenth year, and within a week of her birthday she was safely settled at Conyngton, and, in spite of the grim spectre of war which brooded over the land, happier than she had ever been in her life.

Yet it was by no means a life of leisured ease. Old Miss Mary had died two months before, and many of the duties which had been hers now fell upon Charity's shoulders. The squire and his wife, and even Darrell himself, watched her with some anxiety, but soon found that there was no cause for uneasiness. Charity throve upon responsibility. Her restlessness and boundless energy, which hitherto had made her wild and unpredictable, were directed now towards meeting the challenge of her new life, and though inevitably she made mistakes, she made them only once, and accepted correction and reprimand with a good grace.

"You are growing up, little one," Darrell teased her on one occasion. "I fear the merry madcap we once knew has gone for ever."

She made a laughing retort, but what he said was true in more ways than one. Her new maturity of outlook was matched by physical development, and the gown of amber silk which had been new on the day Darrell brought home his bride was short now in the skirt and uncomfortably tight in the bodice. Charity would always be slender, but the thinness her aunt Elizabeth had so deplored was giving place now to a softer outline, just as the childishness was fading from her face. There was not, nor could ever be, prettiness in those strongly defined features and heavily browed dark eyes, but it was a face at which many people looked twice.

On a hot, still afternoon in the last week of August, Charity happened to be passing through the Long Gallery. Sunlight slanted in at the tall windows, so that the arms of the Conyngtons, wrought in stained glass in each one, glowed like vast jewels and patched the oaken floor with colour. At first she thought the great room was empty, but as she approached the farther end she saw that Darrell and Alison were sitting on one of the window-seats, and that Alison was weeping.

At first Charity was not greatly surprised, for Alison

74

often wept nowadays. Her longing for a child was to be fulfilled at last, but though she was overjoyed at this granting of her dearest wish, her health from the very start of her pregnancy had caused those about her grave concern. Charity, supposing that she felt unwell, went briskly forward, and then Darrell heard her footsteps and looked towards her, and something in his face brought her to a sudden halt. For an instant she stood transfixed, with caught breath and suddenly pounding heart, and then went forward again, more slowly. Her eyes met his, and somehow there was no need to put her question into words.

"A messenger from Alison's brother has just reached us," he said in a low voice. "The King set up his Standard at Nottingham on the twenty-second day of this month."

Charity drew a deep breath, trying to subdue the trembling that had seized her. The raising of the Royal Standard was the ancient call to arms, and though the summons had been long expected it still struck her with a cold sense of shock. She said, in a voice scarcely louder than a whisper, and with only the faintest inflection of inquiry:

"You will go?"

He nodded, his gaze still holding hers. Between them Alison wept softly and desolately, her face hidden. "As soon as our people can be gathered together," he replied quietly. "It will not take long. The preparations are already made."

Charity bowed her head and stared at the coat of arms painted in sunlight and colour on the floor at her feet. Of course the Conyngtons would not hold back. All through the summer Darrell and his father had worked untiringly, gaining the support of those willing to fight for the King, spending lavishly to arm and equip every man they could.

They with their servants and dependants, their neighbours with theirs, would ride to swell the ranks of the Royalist army. There was scarcely a house, proud or humble, for miles around which would not make some contribution. Only the Moat House held aloof, its son committed to the Parliamentary party, its master and his men turning a deaf ear to the demands of loyalty and going doggedly about their usual tasks.

"Darrell, for the love of pity, do not go!" Alison lifted her head, the tears pouring down her cheeks, her voice choked and quavering with sobs. "Do not leave me at this time of all others."

"Dearest, I must! It is my duty and my right," he replied gently, clasping one of the little hands that clutched piteously at his doublet. "We have long known that soon or late this day must come. You must have courage! For my sake, and for the sake of the babe you carry."

Charity turned abruptly away and walked on along the Gallery. She was fond of Alison, and in a calmer mood would have pitied her, but at that moment all gentler emotions were swamped by anger. If a man must ride away to war, she thought, his wife should hide her terror and her tears, and bid him farewell with a pretence of bravery. She should not lay a heavier burden upon him with protests and lamentations.

The next few days were busy ones at Conyngton. Alison was prostrated and took to her bed, but Lady Conyngton, calm and pale, took command of all the necessary domestic preparations, while Charity, flying hither and thither at her behest, had no leisure to think of anything but each new task as it presented itself.

At last, however, all the preparations were completed, and for the first moment since the news had reached them she found herself with time on her hands. It was late and she should have gone to bed, but the old, familiar longing to be out of doors laid hold upon her, and she slipped quietly out into the gardens.

It was a warm, breathless night, heavy with all the sweet scents of summer. The moon sailed a cloudless sky, and in its silver light every leaf and flower hung motionless. The fanciful shapes of clipped yews laid their shadows on smooth lawns, a fountain tossed its shining plume aloft, and in the woods between Conyngton and the Moat House a nightingale was singing. The house, the gardens, the surrounding countryside, were wrapped in a mantle of such absolute peace it seemed inconceivable that in the morning men would go thence to make war upon their own countrymen.

Charity sat down on a stone bench near the fountain and let the stillness of the night wash over her. Slowly her mind ceased to fret over the possibility of some essential task left undone, while all thought of the morrow and of the sadness of farewell receded to an immeasurable distance. This was a moment of peace and beauty suspended between the cares of one day and the next, perfect and inviolable. When a footstep sounded nearby and Darrell came through an opening in the great yew hedge she felt no surprise. The magic of the night had drawn him from the house as it had drawn her.

He sat down on the bench beside her, and for several minutes they listened without speaking to the splash of the fountain and the faint, far music of the nightingale. Darrell was looking towards the house; Charity's own glance turned in the same direction and she caught her breath in wonder, for though she had seen Conyngton in all seasons and at every hour of the day, she had never seen it look as beautiful as at that moment. Set on its terrace above the sleeping gardens, bathed in moonlight which turned its walls and many-gabled roof to silver and set the great windows flashing like diamonds, it had the magical quality of a fairy palace. She was not surprised that when at last Darrell spoke there was love amounting to reverence in his voice.

"Conyngton!" he said softly. "To mine eyes the fairest place on earth. I go to fight for Church and King, yet I know that when battle is joined 'tis of this I will be thinking, this house and those who dwell in it. That is my ultimate loyalty, transcending all other. The star by which I set my course, and which, if God so wills it, shall one day guide me home again."

"I would I could go with you!" A passionate earnestness throbbed through Charity's whispered words. "I would I were a man, that there might be one Shenfield at least to bear arms for the King! Oh, Darrell, it shames me so that *my* family should be the only one in the village to hold back!"

"Each man must act according to his conscience," Darrell reminded her gently, "and none question *your* loyalty, I'll stake my life!" He paused, and a smile glimmered in his eyes as he studied her distressed and angry face. "Though God knows I could find it in my heart to echo that wish of yours, for I'll swear no man could have a more true and valiant comrade-in-arms than you would be."

"I would not hang back, I promise you," she replied with spirit, "but wishing is so much empty folly, and the will to fight is alone not enough. Because I am a woman there is nothing I can do."

"There is much," he said quietly, with a swift return to

gravity. "Do you think that the lot of the women who wait at home is so much easier than that of the men who march away? My father and I take with us every man young and strong enough to bear arms, but the work they have been used to do will not go with them. Our kinsman, Nicholas Hallett, comes also, and stewardship of the estate will fall once more on the shoulders of old James Partridge, whose place Nicholas came here to take. He will need help, I have no doubt. My father leaves much of the business of the estate in my mother's hands, but her health will not support the burden unless you give her all the aid you can. No, little one, though you may not ride beside me, sword in hand, there are many things you can do to help us, and so, if only indirectly, to help our cause."

"I will do anything in my power! You know that!" she replied fiercely. "These things you have spoken of I will remember and strive to do. I would there were more!"

"There is one thing more," he said after an instant's hesitation. "To me the most important of all. 'Tis Alison. With her mother and sisters far away, she is lonely and frightened and takes my going too much to heart. She loves and depends on you, so help her if you can to keep a cheerful spirit, and care for her, and for the child when 'tis born. Will you do this for me, Charity?"

She nodded, and put her hand into his, gripping it hard. "You know I will, Darrell. Alison and her baby shall be my dearest charge and foremost concern, whate'er betide, until you come home again. I give you my most solemn promise on that!"

The promise was still in her mind next day when she stood with Lady Conyngton and Alison on the terrace to bid the men farewell. The bright sunlight of early morning flooded the scene, warming the smooth flagstones, gleaming on the glossy coats of the horses, on the gay liveries and the plumed hats. The ranks of the men who were going with Sir Darrell filled the broad forecourt in front of the house, and more would be assembling in the village and at appointed meeting-places along the way. At the foot of the terrace steps a little group of riders was already mounted, and grooms held horses for Sir Darrell and his son. There were women present, too, wives and sweethearts, snatching a few last moments with their menfolk, and children who chattered excitedly or stared about them in silent wonder. At the windows of the house and in the great doorway clustered more women, and the men too old to fight, but all held back from the space at the head of the steps where their master and his son stood with the three ladies.

Sir Darrell and his wife had said their farewells in the privacy of their own apartments, and whatever anguish they felt at parting was known only to themselves. Lady Conyngton had come forth on her husband's arm, pale but very calm, and now stood leaning on a gold-handled stick while first he, and then their son, took formal leave of her.

Charity, standing a little apart, felt a surge of love and admiration as she watched her. Frail, ill, left to bear alone the crushing responsibilities of a great estate while her husband and only son rode off to war, she yet held herself erect and dignified, and looked with pride at the brave company before her.

With Alison it was a very different matter. Her waiting-woman had dressed her carefully and arranged her hair, but she was weeping and distraught, her eyes swollen and ringed with dark shadows, her whole body shaken with sobs. Charity, seeing the way she clung to Darrell, and the distress in his face as he tried to soothe her, was obliged to force back a rising irritation.

Sir Darrell went down the steps and mounted his waiting horse, but when his son would have followed, Alison uttered a despairing cry and clung to him more tightly than before. He cast a glance of agonized appeal at Charity, and she stepped forward and took the other girl gently by the shoulders.

"Alison, calm yourself, I beg! You do yourself no good by this distress, and do but make Darrell's going the harder." Alison paid no heed, and Charity added in a low voice: "In mercy's name, Darrell, go! It is the kindest way."

He nodded, his face white with distress, and, forcibly disengaging Alison's clinging hands, put her into the younger girl's arms. His hand caught Charity's in a quick, hard grip and he said softly:

"God be with you, little one!"

"And with you, Darrell!" Sadness and fear were clawing at her, but she held her head high and made herself smile at him before he turned away.

He ran down the steps and swung into the saddle, and the horses began to move off towards the gatehouse. When they reached it both Darrell and his father drew rein and looked back, and Charity, bending her head towards the drooping figure in her arms, said in a savage whisper which no one else but Lady Conyngton heard:

"Look up! Look up and smile! Give him at least that memory to carry away."

But Alison paid no heed, and it was Charity herself who smiled and waved in response to Darrell's hand lifted in farewell.

The horses went clattering and jingling beneath the gatehouse and out into the sunlight beyond, and the men on foot tramped after them. The women and children streamed away, too, and in a few minutes the forecourt which had been full of movement and colour lay deserted, with only the white wings and soft cooing of the doves to disturb its stillness.

Lady Conyngton stood motionless at the head of the steps, her hands clasped before her on her stick, the summer breeze stirring the greying hair about her white face where the lines seemed suddenly more deeply graven, and Alison still wept with her head on Charity's shoulder.

The company of men was receding into the distance along the track which crossed the park towards the village, the sound of their going becoming fainter with every passing moment, and at last Lady Conyngton stirred and uttered a deep sigh.

"They are out of sight now," she said in a low voice. "Come, my dears, let us go in!"

6

The Winter of Sorrow—I

The departure of the men from Conyngton was followed by many anxious days for those who remained. They knew that Sir Darrell had intended leading his men to join the Marquis of Hertford in Somerset, where sporadic fighting had already broken out, but beyond that their certain knowledge did not go, though there were many rumours. Plymouth had declared for Parliament, and Charity, paying to the Moat House one of the duty visits upon which Lady Conyngton insisted, found an atmosphere of gloom prevailing there. Mrs Shenfield had been cast into despair by this complete severance from her son and her brothers, while her husband, plainly uncertain where his true loyalty lay, had withdrawn into a mood of sombre abstraction. From her cousin Sarah, Charity learned that many of the younger men living or working on Jonathan Shenfield's estate had slipped off to join Sir

Darrell's company as it marched away, and those who remained were sullen and resentful.

As Darrell had foretold, there was work in plenty to occupy the minds and hands of those who remained at home. The call to arms had come before the harvest was wholly gathered, and there were many other preparations to be made for winter, preparations which this year gained an added urgency from the uncertainty of the times. There was not a house, from Conyngton itself to the humblest cottage, where the absence of the young, able-bodied men did not make itself felt. So many had gone, and who could tell when, if ever, they would return? Those who were left toiled doubly hard, their hearts heavy with dread.

It was on All Hallows' Eve that the first news reached them. At Conyngton evening prayers had been held as usual in the little chapel, and afterwards, as Lady Conyngton with Alison and Charity was passing through the Great Hall on her way to her own apartments, a sudden, heavy knocking sounded upon the main door of the house. After a moment of startled silence her ladyship moved slowly to a chair by the fireplace and signed to the white-haired old steward to see the summons answered. With a manservant at his heels he went through to the vestibule, while other members of the household who had followed the ladies from the chapel gathered in whispering groups, awaiting they knew not what.

There was a brief pause, a murmur of voices, and then a man came slowly and wearily into the Hall. It was Nicholas Hallett, Sir Darrell's cousin, who had come to Conyngton three years before to be his steward, and who had ridden with him to fight for the King. His clothes were travel-stained and his face drawn with fatigue. In a silence broken only by the sound of his spurred boots against the floor he advanced towards Lady Conyngton and bared his head and bowed.

"Give you warm greetings, cousin!" Her voice was calm, though her hands gripped the arms of her chair so hard that the knuckles showed white. "What tidings do you bring?"

He hesitated, looking not at her but at the hat he held, and finally said slowly: "My lady, there has been a great battle in Warwickshire, at a place called Edgehill. The King, advancing upon London, found the Earl of Essex and his Parliamentary forces hard upon his heels, and, fearing to be caught 'twixt them and the troops in London, turned and attacked."

A deathly hush had fallen upon his hearers, and every ear was strained to catch his words. Lady Conyngton said, still in that same calm voice: "We pray that by God's grace victory was granted to His Majesty."

Hallett shook his head. "Madam, neither to His Majesty nor to his enemies. After the battle Lord Essex withdrew towards London, the King to Banbury and thence to Oxford. It was a fierce and bloody fight. At least five thousand men lay dead upon the field when all was done."

He paused again, and Alison, who, clinging to Charity, had been staring at him in ever-growing alarm, could endure the suspense no longer. In a voice which rose jaggedly towards hysteria she cried the question foremost in her mind.

"What of Darrell? What of my husband? Has any harm befallen him?"

"Content you, madam. He is safe in Oxford." Hallett turned to her with what seemed to Charity something like relief. "He sustained a slight wound at Edgehill, but now mends apace. He gave me a letter to carry to you."

With a sob of relief she buried her face in her hands and sagged against Charity, who guided her to a chair and beckoned her waiting-woman to her. Her own relief was no less, but some instinct told her that Hallett had yet more to tell.

"For my son's safety I give thanks," Lady Conyngton said slowly, "but what of my husband?" Hallett did not immediately reply, and she rose from her chair, tension sounding for the first time in her voice. "For the love of God, Nicholas, tell me! What of Sir Darrell?"

With a sudden movement he flung aside the hat and dropped to one knee before her, catching her hand in both his own. His words, broken with grief, yet reached clearly to everyone in the Hall.

"God give you strength to bear your loss, my lady! Sir Darrell died as gallantly as he had lived."

Every vestige of colour fled from Lady Conyngton's face, leaving it ashen grey, and her eyes widened in disbelief. Her lips parted, and she spoke her husband's name in a harsh, terrible whisper. Charity moved anxiously forward, but it was Hallett, starting to his feet, who caught her ladyship's frail figure as it slid limply to the floor. The horrified silence was shattered suddenly as one of the younger serving-maids broke into frightened weeping.

It was the following day before Charity had an opportunity to question Nicholas Hallett, for she had followed the servants who bore Lady Conyngton to her bedchamber, and, desperately frightened but doing her best to conceal it, kept vigil beside her throughout that dreadful night. The widow neither spoke nor wept, but Charity, whose own heart was heavy with sorrow and with dread, could dimly comprehend that her grief was too deep and cruel to find relief in tears.

When at last the house began to stir to wakefulness again she yielded her place at the bedside to Lady Conyngton's waiting-woman and went wearily in search of Hallett. She found him in earnest consultation with James Partridge, but as soon as she had replied to their anxious questions about her ladyship with such reassurance as she could, the old steward went away and left the two of them alone. Nicholas looked at Charity with some concern.

"My child," he said kindly, "you should be in your bed. You are nigh dropping with weariness."

She shook her head. "I will rest presently. Mr. Hallett. you said last night that Darrell's wound is mending. Did you speak truly, or just to reassure his wife?"

"I spoke truth," he replied quietly. "He took a sword-thrust in the thigh, but 'tis an injury more irksome than dangerous. I doubt not he will be on his feet again when I return to Oxford."

"Do you go back there soon?"

"As soon as I have discharged the task he gave me." Hallett paused, regarding her with a faint frown, and then added abruptly: "The Oxford colleges have melted down their plate to provide money for the King's cause, and many private citizens are following this example. Sir Darrell bids me see to it that the Conyngton plate is put to like use."

"Sir Darrell?" Charity repeated, and then paused, realizing that Darrell bore his father's title now. Then the full impact of Hallett's words came home to her, and she said incredulously: "Melt down all that beautiful silver?"

He nodded. "His Majesty is in desperate need of money. The Roundheads have all the wealth of London at their command, and of other large cities also, but though the King's supporters give generously, their chief wealth is in land and its resources and cannot be speedily realized."

"What other cities, sir?" she asked after a moment's silence. "We have heard so many rumours."

Hallett sighed. "Besides London and Plymouth, the Roundheads hold Hull, Bristol, and Gloucester—all the principal ports. The Fleet, too, has declared for Parliament, so that whatever aid comes to us from overseas must run the blockade of enemy ships."

"But there are many loyal to the King, are there not?" she asked in a shocked voice.

"Aye, many, especially in the north and west of England, and in Wales, but there are many accursed rebels also. The struggle will be long and hard, Miss Charity, make no doubt of that. Edgehill was but the beginning."

"Five thousand dead!" she said in a whisper. "Sir, were any other of our people slain, besides Sir Darrell?"

"Five from the Conyngton lands, to my certain knowledge, and as many again gravely wounded," he replied heavily. "I fear I am the bringer of grief to other houses than this."

"How did you come to the King, Mr Hallett? We thought you in Somerset, with Lord Hertford."

"Why, so we were, but the Roundheads sent the Earl of Bedford against us, and he had seven thousand men to our fifteen hundred. We retreated to Minehead, and while Sir Ralph Hopton rode thence into Cornwall with a hundred and sixty horsemen, my lord Hertford took ship to South Wales with the foot and guns, and we with him. That was towards the end of September. Thereafter we marched to join the King's main army, and so, to our sorrow, to Edgehill."

A silence fell between them, heavy with grief and with memories of the brave, proud parting two short months before. Charity, who had sat down by the table, leaned her elbows on it and bowed her head upon her hands, and Nicholas stood looking down at her. Her composure seemed almost unnatural in one so young. Had he not known her well he might have thought her unfeeling, but he had long since recognized her whole-hearted devotion to the Conyngtons. There was a strength in Charity Shenfield out of all proportion to her years. She would bow before sorrow and misfortune, but she would not break. Darrell, sending his kinsman to bear bitter news to his frail, widowed mother and ailing wife, had said:

"God be thanked that Charity is with them!" Nicholas, watching her now, understood the feeling which had prompted the words.

He took a sealed letter from the breast of his doublet and laid it on the table before her. As she looked questioningly up at him, he said simply: "Sir Darrell bade me give you that."

She looked at the letter for a moment, and then picked it up and rose to her feet. She rubbed her free hand across her eyes, suddenly just a weary child again.

"Thank you," she said in a low voice. "Forgive me, but I am so tired. I must rest for a while, but you will tell me, will you not, if there is aught I can do to help you?"

He assured her that he would, and she went away to her bedchamber. The letter from Darrell, though brief, was eloquent of his affection for her and his dependence upon her to help and comfort his mother and Alison, for he could see no likelihood of his own early return to

Conyngton. She read it through twice, and then went to sleep with it beneath her pillow.

Nicholas Hallett stayed no longer at Conyngton than was necessary to complete the task Darrell had laid upon him, and after his departure a kind of lassitude seemed to settle upon the household. Outwardly Lady Conyngton had recovered a little from the shock of her husband's death, but she seldom left her room now and rose less and less frequently from bed. She had had a long talk with Hallett before he left, but what passed between them no one knew, and she had made no protest at the summary removal of every piece of plate the house possessed. It was Alison who protested, démanding fretfully how they were to contrive without it, but Charity had no patience with such complaining.

"We shall take our food and drink from pewter," she said shortly, "and I doubt neither will taste any the worse for it."

As autumn gave way to winter, however, the three ladies at Conyngton found graver matters than these to think about, for the war, or one aspect of it, was coming dangerously close. The little company of horsemen which Sir Ralph Hopton had led into Cornwall at the end of September had, under his leadership, swelled rapidly into an army of several thousand. He occupied Launceston, and in spite of Parliamentary forces raised in Devonshire, and reinforcements sent from London, his cavalry made repeated raids across the river Tamar into Devon. By the beginning of December he was threatening Plymouth itself, but the Cavaliers had no ships with which to prevent their enemies from sending arms, money, and provisions to the garrison by sea, nor were they sufficient in number to blockade the town. An attempt to secure Exeter was also foiled, and by the end of the year the Royalists had been driven back into Cornwall.

On a cold, bright afternoon, when January was only a few days old, Charity was sitting at Lady Conyngton's bedside, her troubled gaze fixed on the sleeping woman who looked so pathetically small and frail in the vast bed. Charity knew that she was dying. Each day she seemed a little weaker, a little more remote, as though life was slipping from her grasp and she had neither the strength nor the desire to hold on to it. Sometimes it seemed as though she had died on the day Nicholas Hallett came riding to Conyngton with the news of Edgehill.

As Charity sat there a great weight of sadness and of fear seemed to bear down upon her. She had loved Sir Darrell and his wife as dearly as though they had been the parents she had never known, and soon both would be lost to her. Darrell was far away, and Alison clung to her more closely and dependently with each passing day. The fighting which had raged around Plymouth might break out again at any time, and though Conyngton had as yet been unmolested, they had heard of other country houses which had been attacked and pillaged. Charity, trying to face the future squarely, to picture Conyngton with no mistress but Alison, was not far from panic. She felt helpless and inexperienced, totally unfitted to bear the responsibility which she could see must soon be thrust upon her.

When Lady Conyngton awoke she seemed a little stronger, and bade Charity ask Alison to come to her and bring all her jewels. Charity, puzzled but obedient, fetched the other girl from her bedchamber where she had been resting, paying no heed to her complaints at being thus disturbed. Alison was now more than seven months pregnant, heavy and listless, and lived in a constant state of apprehension. She dreaded her coming confinement, was haunted by the possibility of one day receiving news such as Nicholas Hallett had brought to Lady Conyngton, and fearful that the tide of war would sweep back into Devon and the security of Conyngton be shattered by the coming of soldiers. Charity, mindful of her promise to Darrell, did her best to keep up her spirits, but with little success.

When they returned to Lady Conyngton's room she made Alison sit down in the chair by the bed, and herself placed the casket containing the jewels on the embroidered coverlet. Her ladyship nodded.

"Thank you, Charity. Now bring my own jewels to me."

When this had been done, and the second box placed beside the first, she laid one thin, blue-veined hand upon them and spoke very seriously.

"You both know why my son commanded that our plate should be melted down, and better that by far than that it should fall into the hands of some marauding troop of Roundheads. Darrell made no mention of these jewels, but we all realize, I think, that they are the only things of great value left to us which can be readily converted into gold. Therefore they must be bestowed in some safe place known only to we three. I believe all our servants to be loyal, but the fewer to share a secret, the more likely it is to be kept."

She paused, breathing quickly, for the effort of making so long a speech had taxed her failing strength. Charity laid her hand over the wasted one resting upon the jewel-cases and said simply:

"Where do you wish me to hide them?"

"That I do not yet know. It should be somewhere away from this house, for if the Roundheads do descend upon us they will ransack the place from attic to cellar." Alison uttered an incoherent murmur of alarm, and Lady Conyngton's weary glance turned kindly towards her. "Dear child, it may never come to pass. I pray with all my heart that it will not, but we must be prepared."

"Of a certainty we must!" Charity agreed promptly. "I think I know where the jewels may be hidden, if your ladyship will consent." She paused for a moment and then added quietly: "At the Moat House."

"Your uncle's house?" Lady Conyngton was startled. "But he would have to be told."

Charity shook her head. "There would be no need. You remember the old gatehouse by the moat? 'Tis a ruin now and no one ever goes there, but I have climbed to the top, and I know where, at the summit, there is a cavity in the wall which would make an excellent hiding-place."

"It is too far away," Alison said fretfully. "How could we keep watch over them?"

"Better if we do not! To be constantly reassuring ourselves of their safety would be to risk betraying the hiding-place, and there is no one now at the Moat House to go climbing among the ruins. Nurse told me that the last person to scale that tower was my father, and that was nigh thirty years ago."

"The tower will serve very well if the jewels can be placed there secretly," Lady Conyngton said with finality. "Can they, my child?"

"I will take them tonight, if you wish, for the sky is clear and the moon close enough to full to be as bright as day. There is no need to approach the house, and even if

93

the dogs hear me they know me well and will not give the alarm."

"So be it," Lady Conyngton agreed. "Put all the jewels into one box, Charity. It will be easier for you to carry." She turned to Alison, indicating the rings on her fingers, the pearls about her throat. "Those also, my dear! Henceforth you and I will wear no jewellery but our wedding-rings."

Reluctantly, for the pearls had been a marriage gift from Darrell, Alison obeyed. Charity, packing them carefully with the other gems in the larger of the two boxes, said suddenly: "Will it not be remarked, and arouse suspicion, if you no longer wear your jewels?"

"We must say that they have been sold to raise money for the King. Mr Partridge will bear us out in that, for he must be told that the jewels are hidden, although not where they lie." She sighed and closed her eyes. "I am very tired. Let me rest now."

That night, as Charity flitted through the gardens and across the park towards the woods, she was conscious of no fear, but only exhilaration and a sense of adventure. It was very cold. The bare branches of the trees painted a black tracery against the luminous sky, and her breath hung mistily in the frosty air. The brook at the far edge of the woods still ran swift and full, but when she reached the Moat House the broad sheet of water below the crumbling tower lay motionless as a mirror, locked in ice.

Coming into the shadow of the gatehouse, she slipped off her thick cloak and hitched up her skirts to the knee. The jewelcase, wrapped in sacking and securely tied, was already secured by a length of rope about her waist so that her hands were free. She slid it round behind her and went nimbly up the worn and crumbling steps of the tiny spiral staircase in the thickness of the tower wall. It was a precarious climb, for in many places the steps were broken wholly away, and near the top the inner wall also, so that she had to edge her way upwards pressed close to the outer wall. with the black depths of the tower's hollow interior gaping threateningly on one side.

She reached her goal, and here the stonework broadened into what had once been battlements. The bright moonlight showed her the spot she sought, and, kneeling down, she took a little knife from her pocket and hacked through the rope which bound the box to her. Sliding it carefully into the hole, she partially blocked the aperture with a few large fragments of stone. Then, satisfied that her errand was accomplished, made her way carefully to the ground again and a short while later was hurrying back the way she had come.

Arriving at Conyngton, she went straight to her ladyship's room as she had been told to do. The spacious chamber was dimly lit and Charity went forward on tiptoe, not wishing to disturb Lady Conyngton if she had fallen asleep. But the shadowed eyes were open, and as she came into the circle of candlelight the faint voice said with profound relief:

"Praise God that you are safely returned, my child! Is all well?"

"All, madam!" Charity came to the bedside, tossing the cloak back on her shoulders. "The jewels are safely hidden, and none save we three any the wiser."

"You are a brave child, Charity," Lady Conyngton said gently, putting out her hand. "I know not how I should have contrived without you these past months."

"What I did tonight asked little bravery," Charity replied candidly, taking the hand in her own warm clasp. "I do not fear the darkness, or the climb up the tower, and you know, my lady, that I would do far more than that for you if I could. Yet often I *am* afraid, when I think of the war, and of the fighting yet to come, and of what may befall us here at Conyngton. Then whatever courage I have ebbs quite away."

"No, my child, your courage will never wholly fail. That is the comfort to which I cling, the knowledge that when I am gone Alison will still have you at her side. For I have not long to live, my dear! I shall not even be granted a sight of my grandchild. No, you must not grieve for me——" For Charity's fingers had tightened suddenly upon hers. "Death comes to me in the guise of a friend, for dearly though I love my son, and would have loved the babe, the light went out of my life on the day Edgehill was fought."

She paused, and Charity dropped to her knees beside the bed, pressing her lips in anguish against the frail fingers. After a moment Lady Conyngton went on:

"There are many troublous times ahead, my child! Alison is sweet-natured and gentle and good, but she has no strength to face the future alone. You are the strong one, Charity! You must have enough courage and wisdom for both."

"You know that I will do anything in my power!" Charity lifted her head, her eyes bright with tears which did not fall. "Before Darrell went away I promised him that Alison and the baby should be my first concern, and now I make that promise again to you. I pray daily to God that He will grant me both wisdom and courage, that I may keep it."

"Dear Charity!" Lady Conyngton's hand freed itself and lifted to caress the girl's cheek. Her voice was very weary, her eyes already closed. She spoke as though to herself. "I have long loved you as a daughter. It would have been great joy to me could you have been my daughter indeed. You and Darrell! That was my dearest and most secret hope, but a mother has no voice in such matters, and a rich dowry is of more importance than steadfast courage and a loving heart. I dared not speak my wish that you and he should wed. Never—until now!"

The words trailed into silence, but for several minutes Charity did not move. Kneeling by the bed, staring unseeingly into the shadows, she contemplated with wonder the thing which Lady Conyngton had just disclosed, the thought of which had never before entered her mind. She knew that it could never have come to pass, for the heir to a baronetcy and a fortune could not marry a penniless orphan, but just for a moment she pictured herself in Alison's place, and knew beyond all doubt that it would have been the greatest happiness the world could offer her.

7

The Winter of Sorrow—II

Lady Conyngton died a week later, so quietly and peacefully that at first those about her did not realize it. Later, Charity stood by the bed, looking down at the beloved face where the lines of suffering and sorrow had now been smoothed away, and knew that she could not grieve for her ladyship's passing. She was at peace now, and surely reunited with the husband she had loved so dearly. The tears that filled Charity's eyes were for the living. For Darrell, who had lost both parents within so short a time; for Alison and the coming child; and for herself, deprived of wisdom and guidance and the tenderest love she had ever known.

They laid the dead mistress of Conyngton to rest in the little village church, in the vault where generations of Conyngtons had found their final resting-place, and the thoughts of many who mourned her went also to the lonely graves on the wind-swept slopes of Edgehill, where lay her husband and the other men who would come not home again. In that bleak, dead season of the year all the grief and desolation of war bore heavily both upon the beautiful manor house on the hill and the village in the valley below it.

The violence of war was soon to be upon them again. On the nineteenth of January the battle of Braddock Down placed all Cornwall firmly in Royalist hands once more, and the Cavaliers, flushed with victory, pushed on into Devon. They stormed Saltash three days later, and once again Plymouth found itself in danger, but as before the Cornish army lacked the resources for a proper siege. Even to blockade the town was a perilous undertaking, for their positions were of necessity very scattered, and the Roundheads lost no time in gathering a force to relieve the port. Almost exactly one month after the Royalist invasion of Devon this force fell upon Modbury, driving the Cavaliers, inspite of their stubborn resistance, back upon Plympton and thence into Cornwall again.

Throughout that month the inhabitants of Conyngton lived in a state of perpetual apprehension, constantly expecting the forces of one side or the other to descend upon them. Alison in particular wrought herself into such panic at the smallest unusual sound that Charity feared it could do some harm to her or to the baby, and in an attempt to soothe her persuaded the steward to send out trustworthy servants in search of definite news, for the wildest rumours were constantly reaching them. As events fell out, however, it was not one of these messengers who brought the dreaded warning, but twelve-year-old Peter Bramble, the innkeeper's youngest son, with whose brother, Diccon, Charity had talked one glad May morning long ago. On a raw, cold February day he came flying across the park and under the arched gatehouse, to hammer on the great doors and gasp out the news that Roundhead soldiers were approaching.

It could not have happened at a worse time. Charity, who had been directing the work of the maids in the dairy, had just been summoned thence by Alison's waiting-woman. Flushed and anxious, the girl had come hurrying in to clutch her by the arm.

"Miss Charity, will you go to her ladyship? I believe she has come to her time!"

Charity stared at her for a moment, trying to conquer a sudden, overwhelming alarm, and then, with a very fair assumption of calmness, turned away from the staring dairy-maids and said quietly:

"I will go at once. Pray find Woodley, and ask her to come at once to her ladyship's room."

Woodley had been Lady Conyngton's personal maid, a sensible, level-headed woman upon whom Charity knew she could depend. She felt desperately in need of help as she hurried towards the principal part of the house, for though the midwife could be fetched from the village in a very short space of time, Charity knew it was to her that Alison would cling for reassurance and courage.

When she entered the Great Hall on her way to Alison's room Peter Bramble was stammering out his warning to the steward and a couple of white-faced serving-men. Charity heard the one word "Roundheads", and ran across the Hall to grab the boy by the arm.

"You mean they are coming here?"

"Aye, Miss Charity, we heard 'em say so! They stopped at the inn to bait, ye see! Boasting, they were, o' the rich plunder they'd find to Conyngton, and that there were none here to stay 'em. Father bade me steal out and

100

run across the fields to warn 'ee." He broke off abruptly and looked quickly at the steward.

Charity said distractedly: "And her ladyship about to be brought to bed! God's mercy, Mr. Partridge, what are we to do?"

"We must speak them fair, Miss Charity, nor do anything to provoke their anger." The old man hesitated, looking worriedly at her. "These are Englishmen, not monsters! They will surely offer no harm to a woman in her ladyship's situation, Roundheads though they be."

"Roundheads?" The strangled cry of terror and despair brought the whole group swinging round. In the archway which gave access to the Grand Staircase Alison stood clinging to the wall for support, her face ashen-pale, her eyes enormous with fear. Her voice rose hysterically. "Oh, God help me! Not coming here?"

"Alison!" Charity sped across to her, and, putting an arm around her, tried to lead her back the way she had come. "There is no need to be afraid, for Mr Partridge is right. They will offer you no harm. Come back to your room."

"No, I will not! Are you utterly heartless? Am I to bear my child while plundering soldiers ransack the house?" Her wide, feverish gaze turned towards James Partridge, standing in wretched indecision a few yards away. "Summon my coach! Let me escape while there is time!"

"Dear, you cannot!" Charity said earnestly. "Do you wish your child to be born at the roadside? You shall not be harmed, I promise you! Our own serving-men shall stand guard outside your door, though I am persuaded the soldiers will not seek to intrude when they are told how it is with you."

101

"Miss Charity speaks more truly than she yet knows, my lady," Partridge broke in, coming a step or two nearer. "There can be no danger to you or to her, for the leader of the Roundheads is her own cousin, Mr Jonas."

"Jonas?" Charity's voice was sharp with sudden dismay. "Are you certain of that?"

"Young Peter has seen him, Miss Charity. To be sure, 'tis a woeful thing to have him coming thus to a house where he has so often been welcomed as a guest, but there is good mingled with the evil of it. At least he will not suffer his men to use any violence."

Charity paid no heed to this. Though staring at the old man, she was seeing instead a snow-swept landscape of more than a year ago, hearing Jonas's voice made ugly by hatred as he swore vengeance upon Darrell Conyngton. What easier way to fulfil that threat than through Darrell's wife and the child she was about to bear? In the name of war any outrage might be committed, and Charity knew her cousin well enough to realize that he would not neglect such an opportunity to even the score.

"Her ladyship is right," she said suddenly. "She will be better away from here. Have the horses put to the coach, and four men armed and mounted to go with us." She turned to Woodley, who with Alison's own maid had already entered the Hall. "Woodley, look after her ladyship, and you"—this to the other woman—"fetch pillows and blankets to put into the coach. Hasten now!"

"Miss Charity, this is madness!" Partridge protested in dismay. "Where can you go?"

Charity looked at him. "To the one place, Mr Partridge, which if my cousin leads these soldiers will be safe from them. To the Moat House!"

She did not wait to hear any further protests, but left

Alison in Woodley's care and ran on and up the stairs. Before she reached the top another thought occurred to her, and she halted to lean over the balustrade and call to the steward: "Gather up whatever money is in the house, and put it into the coach. We'll leave no more than we must for the accursed rebels! And you, Peter Bramble, go back to the village and bid the midwife to my uncle's house."

She went on, and, reaching her bedchamber, dragged out her thick, scarlet cloak and flung it round her shoulders. Then from the bottom of a chest she took a box containing a pistol, which Darrell had given to her before leaving Conyngton. Long ago, before he went to London, he had taught her how to handle the weapon, and for the past month she had kept it loaded in readiness for just such an eventuality as had now occurred.

Tucking the box under her arm, beneath the cloak, she went quickly from the room, along the wide corridor, through the Long Gallery where the pictured faces of generations of Conyngtons looked down from the walls, and down the broad staircase again to the Hall. As she went, she looked wistfully and lovingly about her, hating the necessity for flight. Her instinctive desire was to bar the doors and hurl defiance at Jonas and his Roundhead soldiers, but she knew that even without Alison to consider such action would be sheer madness. To resist would be to invite attack. The only course was to leave the house defenceless and pray that the invaders would not use it too roughly.

The journey to the Moat House, short though it was, was a nightmare to all who made it. Alison seemed almost demented with terror. They had wrapped her in a fur-lined cloak and then in blankets against the bitter cold, and propped her on pillows, with Woodley beside her to hold her and steady her against the lurching of the coach, but she moaned softly with her head against the woman's shoulder, and now and then cried out in pain. Charity held tightly to the box containing the pistol, silently giving thanks that a spell of cold, dry weather had left the ground hard and firm. The coach jolted agonizingly over the frozen ruts, but at least there was no danger of it becoming bogged down in a sea of mire.

After what seemed an eternity they reached the Moat House, and Charity, leaving Alison to the servants, ran ahead of them into the house. Her uncle and aunt, having seen the approach of the coach with its steaming horses, were in the hall to greet her, and in a few brief sentences she explained the reason for their arrival. Mrs Shenfield seemed overjoyed to learn that her son was in the village, but her husband said sternly:

"If Jonas has come back to make war upon us, Elizabeth, there is no cause for rejoicing. Go look to her ladyship."

Mrs Shenfield seemed about to make some protest, but the servants were bringing Alison into the house and she had no choice but to obey him. Her own servants, drawn by the commotion, had come crowding into the hall, and, beckoning to old Nurse and her own waiting-woman, she ordered the others away in a tone which brooked no disobedience. The women surrounded Alison and bore her off upstairs, and Charity and her uncle were left confronting each other in the empty hall.

Jonathan Shenfield looked at his niece in silence. It was less than three months since their last meeting, but the change which he perceived in her astonished him. Charity was no longer a child. She had faced responsibility and

104

mastered it, and now could not be dismissed as a person of no importance. In an attempt to establish again his former authority he said severely:

"It is to be hoped that Lady Conyngton will take no harm from this most ill-advised journey. You should have known better than to allow her to attempt it at such a time, and with so little cause."

"Let us not seek to deceive each other, sir," Charity replied bluntly. "You know and I know that Jonas hates Darrell Conyngton—and Alison is Darrell's wife. Besides, he comes to Conyngton in expectation of rich plunder, and he will be disappointed. That alone is enough to arouse all his vindictiveness."

Events were to prove her right. Barely an hour later, when Charity had gone to join the other women at Alison's bedside, Jonas came riding up to the door of his home. The orange sash of Parliament was across his shoulder, and four soldiers followed at his heels. He dismounted, tossed the reins of his horse to one of them, and swaggered into the house with the other three behind him. Mr Shenfield met them in the hall, and Jonas swept off his hat and bowed with mock deference.

"Give you good day, sir! I trust I find you well, and my mother also?"

"We are well enough," his father replied shortly. "You come home in strange guise, Jonas, with soldiers at your heels."

Jonas tossed the hat on to the table and began to strip off his gloves. "I come upon business, sir. Parliament's business. It is necessary for me to see Alison Conyngton."

"Who told you that you would find her here?"

"What need to be told? She is not at Conyngton, so they must have had warning of my approach, and Charity is shrewd enough to know where their greatest safety would lie. Where is her ladyship?"

"She is above-stairs. You cannot see her."

"I insist upon seeing her, sir! Her lying servants will not tell me where to find that which I seek, but I fancy her ladyship will be less stubborn. Be good enough to send for her—or must I go seek her myself?"

He turned towards the staircase and then halted again, for Charity was coming slowly down it, looking at him with an expression of profound contempt. She said, in a tone that matched her look:

"What do you desire to know, cousin, that the servants at Conyngton cannot or will not tell you?"

He looked venomously at her, struck, as his father had been, by her new maturity, and infuriated by it. He said baldly: "Where have you hidden the plate and other valuables?"

Charity flung back her head, and her clear, mocking laughter went echoing round the lofty room. "Hidden it, coz? The Conyngton plate was melted down months ago to provide money for the King's cause. 'Tis a course taken by many a loyal household. What need to be served from silver dishes when they would be better employed in providing the means to vanquish rebels?"

His eyes narrowed with the anger she never failed to provoke in him, but her words convinced him as none of the anxious protestations of the servants at the manor had succeeded in doing. Many Royalists, he knew, had sacrificed their family plate, and the Conyngtons would be among the first to follow such an example; but plate was not the only wealth they possessed.

"And their ladyships' jewels? I have seen both of them wearing gems worth a fortune."

"The jewels went the same road. Do you suppose the Conyngton women any less loyal than their menfolk?"

With a suddenness which took her by surprise he strode forward and seized her by the arm, jerking her towards him and digging his fingers with deliberate cruelty into her flesh.

"Do you speak truth, you jade? If 'tis false I give you my word you will regret it!"

Charity did not flinch. She was fully as tall as he, and her eyes looked straight into his with no fear at all, but only scorn in their dark depths.

"Do not try to bully *me*, Jonas," she said contemptuously. "I never have feared you and I never will. You may search Conyngton from roof to cellar but you will find neither plate nor jewels."

He believed her, even though he would not yet admit it, and the belief deepened his already evil mood. But though his expectation of rich plunder, which had been his excuse for leading the Roundheads to Conyngton, was genuine, and the prospect of pillaging the manor had filled him with vicious satisfaction, neither was his most urgent reason for coming. Still gripping Charity by the arm, he said malevolently:

"We shall see what Lady Conyngton herself has to say on that score, and I advise you, cousin, to remember that this is a time of war and that I have soldiers at my command. Now take me to her."

Charity shook her head. "You cannot see her. Even you, Jonas, must surely hesitate to thrust yourself in the presence of a woman in the throes of childbirth."

His hand fell from her arm, and he recoiled a pace as though she had struck him. A sickly pallor overspread his face, and he cast a wild glance at his father as though hoping for a denial of her words.

"Your cousin speaks the truth," Mr Shenfield said shortly in answer to that look, "so in the name of mercy take your men and go!"

As though unaware of what he did, Jonas turned away and stood leaning both hands on the massive table in the middle of the room, his head bowed. For a year now he had brooded over his memories of Alison Conyngton, and having heard of the departure of Darrell and his father, had ridden to the manor expecting to find the women there alone. Now, at last, Alison would become aware of him as a man. He had intended to offer her no violence, though making it clear by his treatment of her servants, and especially of Charity, that he was very much the master. Timid, gentle Alison would be terrified, and he would soothe her fears; she would be grateful for his forbearance and he would take full advantage of her gratitude. It would be a vengeance upon Darrell more complete than he had dared to hope for.

He had pictured it all a thousand times, only to find himself thwarted, first by her flight to the Moat House, and now by the unlooked-for, the intolerably bitter knowledge that she was about to bear a child to the man he hated more than any other living being. Darrell Conyngton's child! The thought aroused in him a jealousy and a disgust so fierce that it was scarcely sane.

"Well, cousin?" Charity's cold, mocking voice flicked cruelly across the rawness of his disappointment and his rage. "Will you go, as your father bids you, or are you so lost to common decency that you mean to add shame and terror to the pain she already has to bear? You are the master here this day. We can do naught to hinder you."

Very slowly Jonas raised his head and looked at her. His face was livid, and his eyes blazed so wildly that she was stabbed by an alarm she scorned to show.

"I will go!" he said in a harsh, unnatural tone. "God send her ladyship a safe delivery, and may she bear a lusty son." He laughed, and Charity shivered suddenly, for his look and his tone made the words sound like a curse. "Aye, a son! An heir for Conyngton!"

He turned, and without another word or a backward glance strode from the house, his three men exchanging uneasy looks as they followed him. Charity remained standing where she was until the sound of their horses' hooves had died away, and then she went slowly up the stairs again, feeling no relief at Jonas's defeat, but only an indefinable sense of impending disaster.

Some hours later, when the early darkness of winter had already closed in around the Moat House, she held Darrell's new-born son in her arms. With the other women—Elizabeth, old Nurse, the midwife, and the waiting-woman Woodley—she stood by the bed where Alison lay, waxen-pale, her silvery-gold hair spread across the pillow, her face beautiful and serene in the ultimate serenity of death. Not all their efforts, and they had each striven to the utmost, had been sufficient to save her. The child was alive—just—but the effort of bringing him into the world had been too much for his frail, frightened little mother. She had lived just long enough to know that she had borne a son.

After a little, Charity turned away and walked across to the window, where, holding the baby in one arm, she stretched out the other hand to draw back the heavy curtain. She knew already what she would see, away above the line of the leafless woods. An angry, quivering glow against the sky which told where Conyngton was burning. She had looked on it already, when a frightened maidservant had come tapping on the door and whispered the incredible tidings. Unbelieving, Charity had sped to the window and flung back the hangings, to see hideous confirmation of the woman's words blazoned against the sky. Had stared and stared, while disbelief gave way to horror and to helpless fury.

The baleful glow was less bright now, but her own grief and anger burned with even greater intensity. So Jonas had taken his vengeance, and the savage mockery of his parting words was made horribly plain. The babe she held had been deprived of his heritage even as he drew his first breath, and Alison's whispered prayer of thanksgiving that she had given an heir to Conyngton, the joy which had transfigured her dying moments, meant less than nothing. And somewhere, far away, was a man who had already given unstintingly for his King, and must now be told that in one cruel day he had been robbed both of his beloved young wife and the beautiful home he had called "the fairest place on earth".

The baby stirred and set up a thin, wailing cry, and Elizabeth Shenfield moved away from the bed and came across to Charity. Putting back the coverings from the red, wrinkled little face, she sighed and shook her head.

"Poor, motherless mite!" she said pityingly. "I will send straightway for Parson Flagge, for 'twould be a grievous thing if the babe were to die unbaptized."

"No!" Charity spoke sharply, drawing the infant away from Mrs Shenfield's hand. "He is not going to die!"

Elizabeth shook her head. "My child, I understand your grief, but do not seek to delude yourself. These are matters of which you know nothing. That babe is too small and weakly to survive for long."

"I say he shall not die!" Charity's voice shook with emotion, and her eyes seemed to blaze against the pallor of her face. She flung out a pointing hand, first to the window and the fading glow in the sky beyond the woods, and then towards the dead woman in the bed. "Look on that, madam, and on that! Your son's work, all of it, for Alison might still be alive had she been left to bear her child in peace in her own home. Your son, who is full of a hatred that only cruel, senseless destruction can satisfy!"

Mrs Shenfield recoiled a pace before the violence of her anger, and from the bedside the other women turned to gape at them in amazement. Charity was breathing quickly. When she spoke again her voice was low and passionate and she clasped the wailing infant to her breast in a gesture fiercely protective.

"Darrell Conyngton has been robbed of too much already! This babe, his son, is all that is left to him. I made Darrell a promise before he rode away, and, God aiding me, I will keep it! He shall find his son waiting for him when he rides home again."

Book Two

1

Charity, the Woman

Charity was sitting under the big willow tree at the far end of the moat, in a spot which had been one of her favourite retreats since early childhood. The ground dipped slightly there, and the tree leaned out over the hollow with its trailing branches brushing the grass and the smooth water, so that, when it was in full leaf, anyone sitting there was hidden in a bower of living green. But this was springtime, the foliage had not yet reached the luxuriance of summer, and through it, as though through a veil, Charity could see the whole length of the pool, the hawthorn trees in flower at the farther end, and the crumbling tower which still kept the secret entrusted to it on a long-past winter's night.

Charity was nearly twenty now, and little outward trace was left of the wayward child she had once been. She was dressed in a dark grey gown with apron and broad collar of white linen, her black hair drawn smoothly back and almost hidden by a close-fitting white cap, so that her clear, olive-tinted skin seemed even darker by contrast. Her expression was composed and calm, a new gravity about the generous mouth, the heavily browed dark eyes more often than not modestly downcast, but just as the sober Puritan dress was alien to her nature and worn at the dictates of discretion, so the air of demure resignation was a mask deliberately assumed to cover a nature which had lost none of its fieriness.

She sat very still, leaning against the grassy bank behind her, holding Darrell Conyngton's little son on her lap. She had been giving him his lessons from the hornbook which she herself had used as a child, but after a little while he had fallen asleep with his head against her breast, and now she was reluctant to move lest she disturb him. Sleep was precious to so delicate a child. Charity had kept the vow so passionately made on the day of his birth, but there had been many times when the feeble flicker of life she cherished with such tender care had been in danger of extinction. Sometimes it seemed to those about her that she kept the child alive simply by sheer force of will and the power of her unceasing, all-enveloping love.

She had been given little enough aid in rearing him. It was true that Jonathan Shenfield, appalled by the events of that day and his son's part in them, had provided a home for the child willingly enough, but his wife had never forgiven Charity for the hard things she had said against Jonas. She had turned her back on her niece and the motherless infant, but had reckoned without the girl's independent spirit and fierce determination that the baby should survive. With the aid of the midwife a wet-nurse was found for him, but it was Charity, with old Nurse to

116

advise and help her, who had taken upon her own shoulders the full responsibility of caring for the child. She had caused him to be christened Darrell, for so the first-born son in each generation of Conyngtons had long been named, and devoted herself to him with a single-mindedness which took no account of her aunt's undisguised animosity.

She looked down at him now as he lay sleeping in her arms, and a smile of profound tenderness curved her lips. Although far too small and frail for his age, little Darrell was a beautiful child. The soft, silky hair framing his face was the true Conyngton colour, the red-gold of autumn beech leaves, but in all else he resembled his mother. The delicate features, the long-lashed, dark grey eyes, the fragile bones—these were Alison's. That he had also inherited her timid disposition was a fact which sometimes troubled Charity almost as much as his physical delicacy, but for the most part she succeeded in persuading herself that this was but part of his babyhood, and that he would grow bolder as time went by.

There was a movement on the bank above and behind her, and though she did not move a sudden tenseness took possession of her, a wariness more on the child's behalf than on her own. Then the willow leaves parted to reveal her cousin Sarah, and Charity relaxed again, merely making a little grimace enjoining the younger girl to be quiet. Sarah nodded and sat down on the grass beside her.

"I guessed that I would find you here," she said softly, "but I supposed that you would be giving Darrell his lessons. 'Tis a shame that my mother allows you so little time to teach him."

Charity shrugged. "He does better when we are hidden

away on our own, with little chance of interruption. As for my aunt, I know that she is irked by our presence at the Moat House, and while we are not by, she cannot find fault with us."

"Now there you are mistaken," Sarah said wisely. "When you are not to be found Mother says that you are idle and secretive."

"And when I am present that I am idle and impudent. The first is preferable to the second, since I do not hear it."

Sarah was silent for a space, looking curiously at her cousin. The two girls had drawn much closer together of recent years, for Sarah was the only one of Jonathan Shenfield's three children who possessed in any degree the light-heartedness which had characterized Charity's own father. She was fifteen now, and enchantingly pretty, with a rosy, heart-shaped face, merry blue eyes, and fair hair which refused to stay confined beneath its prim cap but constantly broke into curls around her cheeks and brow.

In the same way her buoyant spirits rebelled against the austere way of life imposed upon the household by her brother, for Jonas was steadily usurping all his father's authority at the Moat House. Ten months previously, with appalling suddenness, Mr Shenfield had suffered a seizure which left him prematurely aged and a mere shadow of his former self, his hair whitened, the left side of his body partly paralysed. He could no longer walk unaided, or speak with proper clarity, and Jonas, ever the opportunist, had since taken upon himself much of the business of the estate.

"Jonas comes home tomorrow," Sarah remarked at length. "Mother has just received a message from him. For my part, I wish he would stay away altogether, for when he is here 'tis naught but preaching and punishment."

A frown wrinkled Charity's smooth brow. Although the long and bitter war was over, Jonas still spent much of his time in Plymouth. The elder of his two uncles had died in 1644, leaving him a fortune which, in spite of the demands of war, was still considerable enough to make him a person of consequence in the town, and Jonas revelled in his new independence. In Conyngton St John, however, he was hated, and when he passed through the village a stony silence greeted him. The blackened ruins of the manor could not be seen from there, but the thought of them was ever present to recall what he had done. The blow struck that day at the Conyngtons was one which would be neither forgotten nor forgiven.

"Take care, Sarah, that he does not hear you say so," she said warningly at length, "or for you it will mean punishment indeed."

Sarah looked rebellious. She knew that Charity's bitterness towards Jonas far exceeded her own, and she was therefore all the more puzzled by her cousin's meek obedience. Charity was never openly defiant now. She had become quiet and self-effacing, taking her full share of domestic tasks, and, when these were done, devoting herself entirely to the little boy.

"I do not understand you, coz!" she said sulkily now. "You were not wont to be so timorous."

"I have learned discretion, child," Charity replied dryly. "In the past I had good friends close at hand. Now I stand alone, and with this dear charge to think of also." She looked down again at the sleeping child. "One day, Sarah, your brother will be undisputed master here. That is something I dare not let myself forget."

"But long before that happens Sir Darrell will have returned," Sarah protested, adding with less certainty, when Charity did not at once agree: "Will he not?"

"God willing!" Charity said in a low voice. "It is my hope, my constant prayer, but what certainty is left to us in this world save that we must one day leave it?"

Bitterness sounded in her voice, and her eyes were sombre as she stared out across the water, for who, even on that black day when Conyngton was destroyed, could have guessed the disasters which still lay hidden in the future? At first, in spite of local reverses, in spite of the bloody shambles of Edgehill, the Royalist cause had prospered. The Queen had returned from Holland with a considerable train of cannon and ammunition; the King's nephew, Prince Rupert of the Rhine, a famous soldier despite his youth, had hastened to England to command the Royalist cavalry; Charles himself had displayed great courage and unexpected qualities of generalship. By the beginning of 1644 the greater part of the country was behind him, and at his headquarters in Oxford he had a Parliament of his own, composed of those who had fled or been expelled from Westminster. Victory had seemed within his grasp.

But it was not to be. The great Parliamentary leaders, Pym and Hampden, were dead, but one of the last acts of Pym's life had been to lead Parliament into signing a Solemn League and Covenant with Scotland, which brought a Scottish army, at Parliament's expense, into England against the King. Unpopular though this was even among the Roundheads themselves, the Scots tipped the balance in their favour. In the south and west the King at first maintained his position. In the north, in July of 1644, his forces were shattered at Marston Moor in the largest and bloodiest battle of the war.

Nor were their Scottish allies Parliament's only strength. During that same year there had risen to prominence an obscure country squire, Member of Parliament for Cambridge and colonel of the mounted troops of the Eastern Counties Association. With his disciplined, steel-clad troopers, nicknamed "the Ironsides", Oliver Cromwell had mastered Prince Rupert's hitherto invincible cavalry at Marston Moor. At Westminster he resisted the Presbyterian Scots and became the champion of all the more obscure and fanatical Protestant sects. He reorganized the Parliamentary forces and transformed them into a New Model Army, the best-equipped and best-paid, the best-disciplined troops England had ever seen. On June the fourteenth, 1645, at Naseby in Leicestershire, a second shattering defeat was inflicted upon the armies of the King. It was the final, decisive blow.

Now it was 1647, and maytime again, and Royalist England lay broken and defeated. The King, who had earlier placed himself in the hands of the Scots, had been handed over by them to the Parliamentary Commissioners. The Queen was in exile in France, her two eldest sons and her infant daughter with her. The other Royal children were hostages in the power of Parliament.

At Conyngton St John the villagers waited in vain for the squire to come home. The other men had drifted back, those who were left, a pitiful remnant of the brave company which had marched away on that late summer day in 1642. Charity knew that Darrell had come through the war with no serious injury, but when the Royalist troops were disbanded he had gone to Alison's home in Kent. Since then there had been no word from him.

"I cannot understand why he tarries so long away," Sarah said musingly at length. "One would suppose him all eagerness to return."

"Why?" Charity asked bitterly. "His wife and parents are dead, his home in ruins, his estate sequestered. What is there here to lure him back?"

"Cousin, do you need to ask that?" Sarah's tone was shocked. "There is his child, the little son whom he has never seen."

Charity sighed. "The child whose coming cost Alison her life. Darrell loved her very dearly."

"But the babe, poor innocent, cannot be blamed for that! And he is so like her! If only his father could see him!" Sarah leaned forward to look at the little boy. She was devoted to him, and was the only person at the Moat House, besides Charity and Nurse, in whose care he seemed happy. "I cannot believe that to be Sir Darrell's reason for not returning. Perhaps, as you say, it is because of the sequestration of the estate. Charity, does that mean that the Conyngon lands belong to him no more?"

Charity frowned. "It means, I think, that Parliament has seized them, or the greater part of them, and that Darrell can only possess them again on payment of a heavy fine. It is called 'compounding', though I fear that he will never bring himself to make terms with the Roundheads. Parson Flagge explained it to me before he left the village, but I am not sure that I fully understood it."

"That is another shameful thing!" Sarah said indignantly. "Why should our parson be driven from his living and from his house to make way for a sour-faced Puritan?"

"Sarah, have a care what you say!" Charity warned her sharply. "Such thoughts are best unspoken!"

"Oh, I would not speak so to anyone but you! I am not so foolish that I do not know when to guard my tongue. But is it not wicked that a kind and godly old man should be persecuted in such fashion—and that Jonas should applaud it? When I see how close in each other's counsels he and the Puritan preacher are I am ashamed to be his sister."

"To be sure they are close! Neither has any other friend in the village." Charity broke off as little Darrell stirred and awoke. For a space he stared about him, large-eyed and solemn, but when Sarah held out her hands to him his face broke into an enchanting smile. He scrambled from Charity's lap and she rose to her feet, brushing a few blades of grass from her skirts.

"Come," she said. " 'Tis time we went within."

Sarah got up, too, and with the little boy between them, clinging to their hands, they climbed the bank and went slowly towards the house. The sun felt warm on their shoulders, and the rich grass through which they walked was scattered with buttercups; a swan glided dreamily across the surface of the moat. To Charity there was something strangely sad in the fact that this peaceful place remained unchanged when so much else that was beautiful and dear had passed away. When they reached the hawthorn trees she paused and looked up at the flowering branches, pink and white against the deep blue of the sky.

"Oh, for the old days," she said softly, "when we used to go a-maying! Before the maypole was torn down and the mayday revels condemned by Jonas and his kind as a sinful abomination." She was silent for a moment, and then as she glanced sidelong at Sarah, the old, mischievous Charity peeped for an instant through the decorous mask. "I often marvel, cousin, that those who profess to be so righteous can detect such evil in simple things."

Sarah laughed, and little Darrell chuckled too, sharing her mirth without understanding it. He pulled his hands free and ran ahead of them until they came to the house, but at the door he halted and then returned to Charity, clutching her hand again.

She stooped and lifted him in her arms, a familiar ache tugging at her heart, for it was always thus. No matter how merry he seemed out of doors, a shadow seemed to touch him as soon as he entered the house, as though he knew that he was accepted there only on sufferance. It was at those times more than any other that she saw Alison in him. She carried him straight to the nursery she had once shared with her cousins, and which Elizabeth, at her husband's behest, had grudgingly allowed her to make her own domain. There, at least, she knew a measure of freedom, but it was a sanctuary which would not endure for ever.

That evening, when the little boy was asleep, she sat there with Nurse, now her most frequent companion. Nurse was very old, a little, bent woman with a face like a wrinkled apple, but though she could no longer work as she had once done, her faculties remained unimpaired by age. From her seat in the shadows she watched the girl's face as she bent over some sewing in the pool of light cast by the tallow candles on the table, observing the faint frown drawing together the thick brows and the troubled set of the lips. Charity had always been the best-loved of all her nurslings, and she could read without difficulty every emotion mirrored in that dark, expressive face.

"What be troubling 'ee, my chick?" she asked abruptly at last.

Charity sighed and put down her work. "I can hide nothing from you, can I?" she said ruefully. "Nurse, do you realize that little Darrell is four years old? Soon he will need better teaching than I can give him if he is to be educated as befits a Conyngton, and what means have I to furnish him with a tutor? I cannot ask my uncle to provide one. He might consent, but Jonas and my aunt would find some way to prevent it."

"Aye, Master Jonas holds the purse-strings now, more's the pity!" Nurse's tone was disapproving, for she had little patience with Jonas and regarded with scorn his ever-increasing self-importance. " 'Tis true he has no kindness for the little master, and no more has Mistress—more shame to 'em! What harm has he ever done them, the pretty dear?"

"He is Darrell Conyngton's son," Charity replied in a hard voice. "That is the only reason to hate him that Jonas needs." She looked up suddenly to meet the old woman's watchful eyes. "Nurse, there are times when I am mortally afraid! My uncle is our only safeguard, and his health grows more feeble week by week. What will become of us, little Darrell and me, when he is dead?"

"Y'd not lack food nor shelter, either of 'ee," Nurse said soothingly. "Not while one roof still be standing in Conyngton St John."

"Oh, we have good friends in the village, I know!" Charity laid aside her sewing and got up to move restlessly about the room. "But they have little enough for themselves now, poor souls, and besides, it would not be fitting for the heir of Conyngton to grow up in cottage or farmhouse. If only I knew what best to do! Oh, why does Darrell not come home? I am so weary of bearing this burden all alone."

2

Jonas

She was to have news of him the very next day, from the most unexpected source of all. Jonas arrived at the Moat House midway through the afternoon, but though Charity was aware of the bustle which always heralded his arrival, she did not see him until that evening, when the household assembled in the hall for prayers. She had learned that it was best to avoid him as much as possible, lest the bitterness she felt, and which his attitude towards her and the child never failed to quicken, betrayed her into the indiscretion of quarrelling with him. So she greeted him with quiet civility before moving to her accustomed place, which was nicely calculated to lie somewhere between the family and the upper servants.

Jonas himself conducted the prayers, and Charity, looking at him as he stood waiting for the servants to take their places, thought that he seemed to be more than ordinarily pleased with himself. He was now in his early twenties, a stocky, thickset young man, handsome of feature yet with something in his face which was curiously repellent. Perhaps it was the complete lack of humour, and the cruelty which now inhabited eyes and lips and which was a reflection of the bigotry and intolerance of his nature. Jonas was a man of consequence now in his own world, and as his influence and authority grew, so also grew his harshness towards those less fortunate.

Sensing that someone was watching her, Charity turned her head and found herself looking straight into the pale eyes of Daniel Stotewood, Jonas's body-servant. Stotewood was a Plymouth man, and being bound by none of the ties of blood or custom which united even the Shenfields' servants with the rest of the village folk, was regarded by them with suspicion. He was a lanky young man with a sallow face and straight, gingery hair, and a perpetual air of mock humility. Charity detested him and he knew it. There was nothing he liked better than to be able to carry tales concerning her to his master.

The prayers were long, and full of the wrath and fury so dear to the devout Puritan, but Charity had long since learned to turn a deaf ear to them and withdraw secretly into her own private devotions. She prayed, simply and with complete faith, in the old, beautiful words she had learned as a child, and, as always, found in them strength and consolation. Afterwards she would have bidden her uncle and aunt good night and returned to the nursery, but to her surprise Jonas detained her.

"Tarry a moment, cousin! I have that to say which may perchance interest you."

Charity paused and looked at him, as much in distrust as in surprise. Jonas rarely troubled himself to address her, and now there was a note in his voice, and a curiously triumphant expression in his eyes, which filled her with disquiet. Scorning to show it, she inclined her head in assent and walked back to join the group around the fireplace. Jonas turned to address his father.

"Sir, it gives me pleasure to inform you that I have lately been at some pains to increase the extent of the land we hold. I have purchased all that to the north and east of our boundaries, from Whitethorn Farm to High Wood."

An instant of complete silence greeted his words, and then Charity said in a shaking voice: "I do not believe it! That is Conyngton land."

"You are mistaken, cousin!" Jonas had been watching her closely and now spoke with undisguised satisfaction. "It *was* Conyngton land. Your friend Sir Darrell has sold it to me."

Charity stared at him, realizing the source of his satisfaction and the desire that she should be a witness of his triumph. She said unsteadily: "It cannot be true! Darrell would not part with one acre of his inheritance to you."

"He had little choice," Jonas retorted brutally. "The days when a Conyngton could ride roughshod over whomsoever he pleased are long since past. The only means by which Darrell Conyngton could raise sufficient money to compound for his lands was by selling a goodly portion of them. I offered the best price, and he was glad enough to pocket his pride and accept."

Sarah stretched out her hand to take Charity's, clasping it tightly. She said quickly, before the elder girl could speak again: "Then you have seen Sir Darrell, Jonas?"

"No, I have not seen him. He stays in London, whither he went to make terms with Parliament. Our business was conducted by the lawyers."

Charity pressed Sarah's fingers in return and then withdrew her hand. Beneath the shock and disbelief a tiny hope had sprung up in her heart at Jonas's news, but now Sarah had asked the question she had lacked the courage to voice, and hope had perished again. If her composure were not to desert her utterly she must get away at once from Jonas's mocking grin, his mother's malicious gaze. She made a little gesture of despair, and went slowly towards the stairs.

For a long time that night she lay wakeful, staring into the darkness, thinking of Darrell and of the straits to which he had been reduced, her heart aching for the grief he must feel at being obliged to part with land his family had owned for generations. It was small wonder that he was reluctant to return, but if he did not, what would become of his son? Jonas still hated Darrell, hated the affection with which, even in his absence, he was regarded in the village, and resented the deep, unspoken antagonism which he himself had provoked there. His acquisition of part of the Conyngton lands might merely whet his appetite for further reprisals, and though Darrell was beyond his reach, he might see in the child a satisfactory substitute for the father.

Proof that these fears were not entirely groundless was forthcoming a few days later. Charity and Sarah, taking little Darrell with them, had gone to the meadow by the brook to gather the cowslips which grew in profusion there, and which had many uses in stillroom and kitchen. Returning home with their baskets full of sweet-scented golden flowers, and with the child, tired and grubby, clinging to their hands, they came face to face with Jonas near the house. He stood barring their way, arms akimbo and feet wide-planted, looking at the little boy. Darrell's face was dirty and his holland smock stained with mud, and one small, hot hand clutched a bunch of wilting cowslips.

"The heir of Conyngton!" Jonas said with a sneer. "Roaming the fields like a gipsy brat when he would be better employed in minding his books. Why are you not at your lessons, sirrah?"

Thus addressed, in a loud, hectoring voice, by one of whom he was at all times terrified, the child stared wide-eyed for a moment and then burst into tears, burying his face against Charity's skirt. Sarah said indignantly:

"Pray do not bully him, Jonas! You know that he is afraid of you."

"By all accounts he is afraid of his own shadow! A rare jest, is it not, that the proud Conyngtons should have spawned this snivelling weakling?" He spoke again to the child, his voice more menacing still. "Be silent, boy! Upon my word, 'tis time someone flogged a trifle of spirit into you."

"That would not serve!" Charity, who had dropped to her knees to comfort Darrell, looked up at Jonas, her eyes brilliant with anger. "You should know that, cousin! It never served with you."

An angry flush darkened his face, but she saw a gleam of triumph in his eyes which warned her of the dangerous ground she trod. With an effort she mastered her own feelings and got up, saying in a calmer tone:

"Sarah, will you take Darrell indoors to Nurse? Tell her that I will come directly."

Sarah looked uneasily from her brother to Charity, and then took the little boy by the hand and led him away, talking softly and reassuringly to him as they went. When they were out of earshot Charity drew a long, steadying breath and looked again at Jonas.

"That you hate his father I know," she said in a low voice, "but in the name of pity, Jonas, can you not show a little kindness to the child? How can you bear so bitter a grudge against that poor, motherless mite?"

For a few moments Jonas continued to regard her, his expression sombre. Though Charity could not know it, her words probed a wound which for years had festered unhealed, suspected by no one. His boyhood passion for Alison Conyngton had been innocent enough, but a sense of guilt, fostered by the harsh faith he had embraced, had continued to torment him until it assumed in his mind the magnitude of a mortal sin. In Plymouth he was able to thrust it aside, but as soon as he returned to the Moat House there was her child to stir the agonizing memories to life again. Had little Darrell's likeness to his mother been complete, Jonas might have looked more kindly upon him, but he could not endure the mockery of seeing dead Alison's sweet face crowned by the red-gold Conyngton hair, to remind him that here was not only her son but the son of the man he hated so bitterly.

"The child has no claim upon us," he said roughly at last, "and now that the wars are over should be sent to his father. The Moat House is growing overfull of homeless orphans."

Charity shook her head. "No, Jonas," she said quietly. "Little Darrell belongs to Conyngton St John. The manor may lie in ruins, but this is still his home, his birthright, and one day his father will come to him."

"And what if he does?" Jonas retorted mockingly. "Already Darrell Conyngton's lands have dwindled, and as time passes he will have no choice but to sell more. How much of the inheritance you prate of will be left for the boy by the time he comes to manhood?"

She stared at him, cold dismay taking possession of her as she realized at last the extent and ruthlessness of his purpose. "So now we have the truth of it," she said bitterly. "In spite of all the wrongs you have done him, your thirst for vengeance is still unslaked, and now you mean to use your uncle's wealth to finish the wicked work the Roundhead soldiers began for you four years ago."

He grinned at her. "Gold, cousin, can be a more deadly weapon than steel. I am a wealthy man, and shall be wealthier yet, and I will ruin Darrell Conyngton as I swore to do when he humiliated me and made me a laughing-stock. I will teach him what it is to be disregarded and set aside, to be a creature of no account."

"Cousin, you still crow louder than any cock!" Charity's voice was scornful. "There is one thing you have overlooked, and that is the love and respect the Conyngtons command. You may possess yourself of the last acre of Darrell's land, drive him from the village, from Devon, even from England itself, but you can never make yourself squire of Conyngton St John. That is a place which only he or his son can fill."

"You think *I* crave the regard of these poor, misguided fools?" Jonas said contemptuously. "I know how I am looked upon in the village, and how they dote on the puling brat when you carry him from house to house. 'The little master' they call him! Well, Mistress Impudence, the day will come when you and they shall learn what it is to have a master indeed. I will turn the people of this parish into the ways of righteousness despite themselves."

"In honesty's name, Jonas, have the courage of your own villainy!" she retorted sharply. "Mayhap you *will* succeed in making good your threats, but if you do it will be to satisfy your own jealousy and greed, and not for our salvation. Venom such as yours springs not from God but from the devil."

She brushed past him before he could reply, and walked quickly towards the house. Her heart was pounding and she was trembling from head to foot with anger, but she was frightened too. There seemed to be every chance that Jonas would succeed in his purpose. His boast that he would be wealthier yet was no idle one, for the uncle who was now his partner had no other heir, while Jonas himself, so Charity had heard, possessed an unexpected talent for business which promised to make him one of the most prosperous men in Plymouth.

Darrell, on the other hand, like so many devoted Royalists, had poured out his wealth ungrudgingly on behalf of the King. Some of the Conyngton lands had been sold, and some of them mortgaged, long before the fighting was over, and that which remained drained dry of every penny it could provide. The farms and cottages were falling into disrepair, for after the old steward's death—James Partridge had survived the burning of Conyngton by less than a year—there had been no one to handle the business of the estate. All was in chaos, and unless Darrell came home Charity could see no likelihood of it being set to rights.

To her relief there were no disastrous consequences of her quarrel with Jonas, and she realized that he would find far greater satisfaction in allowing her to remain at the Moat House and watch him gradually tighten his hold upon Conyngton St John than he would in turning her out to fend for herself.

The days lengthened, the hawthorn blossom faded, and

the roses came into bloom. Haymaking began, and the sweet scent of new-mown hay hung like incense over the countryside, but though the slow pageant of the seasons unfolded as it had always done, the old joyousness was lacking. A blight lay upon the land. The simple rural customs and festivities in which the Church had joined hands with farmer and labourer were now condemned as lewd, idolatrous practices, for the Puritans were offended almost as much by the beauties of nature as by the sins of the world, and believed that men must be saved from the temptations of both.

At the beginning of June Jonas returned to Plymouth. Charity greeted his departure with relief, for when he was at the Moat House she felt that she had to be constantly on her guard, while little Darrell's timidity increased to an alarming degree. He clung to her so tenaciously that she found it difficult not to neglect the domestic duties Mrs Shenfield heaped upon her, for not even Sarah could persuade him away from her for long at a time. Charity, looking at his pale little face and frightened eyes, felt her heart grow heavy with loving fears, and foreboding of what the future might hold for him.

Early one morning, a week or so after Jonas's departure, she was churning butter in the diary when Sarah peeped round the door. Charity, who knew that the younger girl should have been busy with her own allotted tasks, said with mock severity, not ceasing her own labours:

"What do you here, mistress? It will go hard with you if your mother finds you idle."

Sarah came in and closed the door. Her eyes were sparkling, her cheeks flushed with some suppressed excitement.

"I know," she said as she came across to her cousin, "but no matter for that! Charity, Peter Bramble was here a few minutes since, bearing a message for you." She laid her hands over Charity's as they still grasped the handle of the churn, and her voice shook with the same excitement that lit her eyes. "Cousin, your prayers are answered. Sir Darrell is come home at last."

3

Return to Conyngton

For a few seconds Charity stood utterly still, staring at her. Then she said in a whisper: "Sarah, is this the truth?"

"The truth, as I live! He is at the inn. Peter says he came there last night, after dark, and only his body-servant, John Parrish, with him. They lay there the night, and this morning Abigail Bramble sent Peter here to tell you."

"Abigail sent him?" A faint frown creased Charity's brow. "Did he then bear no message from Darrell himself?" Sarah shook her head, and she added impetuously: "I must go to him, and take the child! Where is my aunt?"

"Busy in the stillroom, and like to be so for an hour or more. You have naught to fear from that quarter, and since I met Peter before he had spoken with anyone else here, even the servants do not know yet what news he brought."

"God bless you, Sarah!" Charity leaned forward and kissed her cousin lightly on the cheek. "Will you run to the stables and ask William to saddle my pony? 'Tis too long a walk to the village for little Darrell."

Sarah hurried away, and Charity, recklessly abandoning the butter, ran indoors and up the stairs to the nursery. Nurse, busy at her spinning-wheel while the child played nearby, looked up with a start, and stared to see the girl utterly transfigured, her cheeks flushed and her dark eyes shining with joy.

"Lord, save us, Miss Charity!" she exclaimed. "What's toward?"

"That for which we have hoped and prayed!" Charity swept the little boy up into her arms and hugged him. "My sweet one, this is a wondrous glad day! Your father is home at last!"

She left Nurse murmuring a prayer of thanksgiving, and, bidding little Darrell be still, for he was tugging at her collar and asking excited questions, she carried him down the back stairs and out into the stableyard. William, the middle-aged groom, was waiting there with the old grey pony, and Charity set the little boy in the saddle and led the pony out of the yard and across the park towards the road.

Once away from the house, Darrell began to chatter eagerly once more, asking innumerable questions and paying no heed to her answers. She had talked to him often about his father, striving to create a picture of Darrell in his infant mind in preparation for the time when they would meet, and in some measure she had succeeded. Now, however, as she listened to his artless prattle, she

138

was conscious of certain misgivings. She had described Darrell as she remembered him, the light-hearted comrade of her childhood, the youth who had ridden away to war so full of high purpose and certainty of the ultimate triumph of the cause he served. What did she know of the man who had come back, defeated and poor, his King a prisoner, his home and family lost? Would a stranger be waiting for them at the inn?

At last the pony's plodding hooves were traversing the village street. Little Darrell had fallen silent now, as though realizing for the first time the magnitude of the occasion and overcome by it, and Charity, too, was aware of a curious stillness within herself, something which was neither gladness nor hope nor fear, yet in some strange way compounded of all three.

When they drew level with the church she saw Dr Malperne, the Puritan parson, coming through the lychgate, and mechanically bade him a civil good day. He nodded in response, but as she walked on along the street she felt his cold gaze following her, and knew that he had paused, a black, crow-like figure, to watch whither she went.

As she lifted the child down from the pony outside the inn, Diccon Bramble emerged. He had lost an arm at Edgehill, and his empty left sleeve was pinned across his breast, but his flaxen hair and wide, slow grin were the same as ever. He beamed at them.

"Good morrow to 'ee, Miss Charity, and to 'ee, little master. 'Tis a great day for Conyngton St John," he greeted them, and at once, by some curious freak of memory, Charity's thoughts flew back to a springtime morning when he had spoken those same words to her.

139

Little more than six years past in time; an eternity away in sorrow and suffering.

Abigail Bramble, Diccon's mother, appeared from the kitchen, wiping her hands on her apron and looking puzzled. "Good morrow, Miss Charity! Be Sir Darrell not with 'ee?"

Charity shook her head, suddenly uneasy. "I have not yet seen him. I looked to find him here."

Abigail's frown deepened. "He rode off afore my Peter returned, and took the road up the hill. I made sure he were coming to the Moat House."

Little Darrell tugged at Charity's skirt. "Is my father not here? You said he would be!"

"No, sweetheart, but he is not far away. Stay with Abby, and I will go fetch him."

She lifted the child and put him into Abigail's arms, and then went out again into the sunshine, knowing with absolute certainty where she would find Darrell. Instead of returning the way she had come, she took the lane to the left of the forge, and when the last cottages had been left behind, struck off to the right, up the hill towards Conyngton. Passing through meadows where the haymakers were at work, she reached the deserted park whence the deer had long since vanished. So she came at last to the ruined gatehouse, and from the shadow of its arch looked across the gardens to the blackened shell of the mansion, rising stark and gaunt amid the lush green summer foliage.

She had been there only once since the burning of the manor, on a day in the following spring, when, feeling it to be her duty to do so, she had gone to see for herself the full extent of the destruction.

What she found left her sick and shaken. Jonas and his

men had done their work with appalling thoroughness, and not only the great house itself, but every outbuilding also, had been looted and burned. The horses were stolen from the stables, the hawks set free, the hunting-dogs slaughtered or driven out. The sheep from the folds, the cattle from the byres, even the poultry and the doves, were scattered or destroyed. In the gardens the fountain lay shattered, the statues cast down from their pedestals, the flower-beds and smooth lawns trampled by careless hooves. Where there had once been constant comings and goings, and all the stirring life of a great household, now was nothing but emptiness and desolation. Overcome with grief, Charity had fled, and never found the courage to return.

Now, after four years, some of the harshness had been blurred by the kindly hand of nature. Trees and shrubs had grown tall in the neglected gardens, flowers had run riot to mingle with grass and weeds, and even on the crumbling, smoke-blackened walls a few living things had found a foothold. Yet, even though leaf and blossom had begun to veil the crude signs of man's destructive fury, their very abundance served to emphasize the devastation, as though field and forest were eager to obliterate all evidence of human endeavour.

For a few moments Charity stood motionless in the archway, feeling again the horror which had engulfed her the first time she looked upon the havoc wrought in this loved place. Then there was a movement beyond some tall bushes away to the right, and she saw that it was a horse, saddled and bridled but left to roam at will, that cropped long grass which had once been a stretch of shaven lawn. She went forward, half eager, half reluctant, across the weed-grown forecourt and up the steps to the terrace and the gaping aperture which had once been the main entrance to the house.

At the head of the steps, on the cracked flagstones, the arms of the Conyngtons, wrought in stone, which had once surmounted the doorway, lay shattered into fragments. She picked her way between them to the threshold and there halted again, frozen into stillness by an emotion so powerful that it robbed her of speech and movement.

In the midst of the ruined hall, his back towards her, a tall man stood bareheaded, as though in the presence of death, and the summer sunlight glowed on hair of reddish gold. His shoulders were bowed, and in every line of that still figure she read an anguish that smote her to the heart. The words he had uttered on the night before his departure rang again in her mind: ". . . this house and those who dwell in it—the star by which I set my course." A compassion so profound that it swept aside all doubt and hesitation welled up within her, and in a gentle voice she spoke his name.

He spun round towards her, and she saw in his face all the anguish of this bitter homecoming. For a second or two he stared, as though he did not recognize her, and then he said in a low, shaken voice:

"Charity! Little one, is it you in truth?"

The sound of the old, loved name upon his lips broke the spell which seemed to bind her. With hands outstretched in eager greeting she sped forward, somehow avoiding the hazards of broken flagstones and the heaps of rubble that littered them, and he caught her in a hard embrace and buried his head upon her shoulder. Her arms about him, her cheek against his hair, she held him as she might have held his little son, sensing his bitter grief, his desperate need for comfort.

After a long moment he raised his head again and looked up and around them at the charred beams and crumbling, blackened stone, the leafy branches thrusting in through broken walls. A violent shudder shook his whole body.

"I had not guessed!" he said huskily. "Though you sent me word of what befell, though I knew all lay in ruins, the truth I find here is beyond my cruellest imaginings."

"I know!" she whispered. "Oh, my dear friend, I know! I would willingly have given my life to prevent this horror, to keep faith with the promise I made."

At the passionate earnestness of those words his gaze returned to her, and it was as though he really saw her for the first time. He slackened his grip and held her a little away to look into her face, and she met the regard with a look equally intent, each discovering in the other the changes the years had wrought.

She knew at once that she would have recognized him anywhere, although the youth she remembered had become a man, taller, broader, looking older than his four-and-twenty years. The likeness to his father was more pronounced, but there was a stern sadness in his face which the elder Darrell Conyngton had never known. It was the face of a man who had endured much, and there was bitterness in the hazel eyes and in the line of his lips. Then he smiled at her, and the sudden softening of his expression recalled with heart-breaking vividness the boy she had once known.

"My dear little sister," he said gently, "think you I do not know how steadfastly you *have* kept faith? Even had I doubted it, which God knows I never did, I could not have spent a night in Conyngton St John without discovering that I was mistaken. And had I not known that I would find *you* here I doubt whether I could have found the courage to return, to face—what has to be faced."

"Darrell!" Charity reached up to set her hands on his shoulders; her voice was very earnest. "This village is still your home, and its people love and respect you as they have always done. No matter what else is lost, that endures. Today there is gladness in every heart because the squire has come home."

A faint frown creased his brow for a moment, and a look she could not interpret flickered in his eyes. Then from somewhere high above them in the decaying walls there was a whisper of sound, and amid a tiny cloud of dust a few fragments of stone rattled down, noisy in the stillness of that deserted place. Darrell glanced sharply round, and his frown deepened.

"There is peril here," he said abruptly. "Some of these walls must be on the verge of collapse. Come!"

With an arm about her shoulders, he led her back to the doorway and through it on to the terrace again. He looked about him at the wilderness the gardens had become, and she saw his face contract with pain.

"I have fought across a dozen counties of England," he said in a low voice, "and I have seen the cruel havoc that war can wreak, but never have I seen aught to equal this. There is more here than the ravages of hostile soldiery. Something almost fiendish, as though the intention were to sweep Conyngton from the face of the earth."

"Perhaps it was," she replied gravely. "There is a kind of hatred which must destroy what it cannot possess."

"Did Jonas, then, hate me so much?" Darrell looked at her in astonishment, almost in disbelief. "God's mercy, Charity! Why?"

She shook her head. "I do not know! Oh, he was al-

144

ways jealous of you, and when you disarmed him and cast his sword into the river he swore that he would make you regret it. I think that was why he led the Roundheads to Conyngton, and yet, when I look back upon that day, it seems that there was something more. When he left the Moat House, whither he had pursued us, he was like a man possessed."

"And so he returned here to pillage and destroy," Darrell said with a sigh. "Well, God knows his hatred must be satisfied by now! He prospers, I am told, grows rich and influential, while I . . ." He gave a curt, mirthless laugh. "I have lost everything."

For a moment she was tempted to tell him the truth concerning Jonas, but compassion triumphed and she held her peace. There would be time enough later to put him on his guard. Already this day had laid too heavy a burden upon him.

"Not everything, Darrell," she said gently after a moment. "You still have the most precious possession of all—your son! He is waiting for you at the inn." She put out her hand in a pleading gesture. "Will you come to him?"

He took her hand in his, and stood for a moment or two looking down into her eyes. Then suddenly he bent his head, and pressed her fingers to his lips.

"What an ingrate I am," he said unsteadily, "to speak as though *your* loyal and loving friendship counted for naught. But though my words be thankless, little one, my heart is not. I know, for Abigail has told me, to whom the child's survival is due. Yes, let us go!"

They did not return to Conyngton St John by the way Charity had come, but went along the grass-grown track across the park to the great gateway. They walked slowly,

Darrell leading his horse, for there was much to say to each other, and the sun was high by the time they entered the village street. Most of the villagers were at work in the fields, or the women about their domestic tasks, so that only the very old or the very young, the infants at play, and the aged nodding in the sun at cottage doors, saw the two go past. They, and one other. From a window of the parsonage Dr Malperne watched them, the slim, dark girl in Puritan dress, and the tall Cavalier with the proud bearing, who walked together in such close and serious conversation.

They reached the Conyngton Arms, and stepped into the cool, whitewashed passage which traversed the house from front to back. At its farther end the kitchen door stood open, and from within came the sound of a clear, childish voice. Charity offered up a brief, silent prayer that little Darrell, so often shy and timid in the presence of strangers, would not be so with his father, and led the way along the passage.

He was standing by the table where Abigail was kneading dough, both hands clutching its edge which reached almost as high as his chin. His face was upturned, flushed with earnestness, the great grey eyes wide and intent as he imparted some childish confidence. Charity heard the man beside her catch his breath, and then say in a whisper:

"Alison!"

The little boy looked towards the door and with a cry of delight started to run to Charity. Then he halted again to stare doubtfully at her companion, but she moved quickly forward and took him by the hand.

"My darling," she said gently, "did I not promise you that you should see your father today?"

Clinging to her hand, he pressed close against her,

looking up wonderingly at the tall man in his Cavalier lace and velvet. Charity held her breath, and at the table Abigail's busy hands were stilled as she, too, watched anxiously. Darrell's face was taut with emotion and for a moment he seemed incapable of speaking. Then he went down on one knee and held out his arms to the child.

"Come, my son!" he said in a shaking voice.

For an instant longer the little boy hesitated, and then he loosed Charity's hand and moved forward, uncertainly at first, and then with a rush which took him straight into the outstretched arms. She let her breath go in a long sigh of thankfulness, and looked down through a sudden blur of tears at the two bright heads so close together, knowing that the vow made in anger and heart-break at Alison's death-bed had not been in vain.

4

The Decision

Charity returned to the Moat House to find herself in deep disgrace. Nurse, who had been hovering anxiously at the door, came out into the stableyard as soon as Charity led in the grey pony, and said softly to her:

"Mistress be in a rare ill humour, my lamb, and screeching for 'ee to be sent to her as soon as 'ee come in. Leave the babe wi' me, and go."

Charity sighed, and lifted the little boy to the ground. "Go with Nurse, my darling, and tell her about your father. I will come directly."

She found her aunt awaiting her in the parlour. Elizabeth Shenfield had grown stout, but the comfortable effect created by her ample figure was belied by her expression, for though she had embraced the Puritan faith and accounted herself a very godly woman, charity and loving-kindness were not among her virtues. She regarded her niece now with an angry glitter in her eyes, for the girl's

148

presence at the Moat House, made inevitable by the destruction of Conyngton, was one of the very few things for which Mrs Shenfield could not forgive her son.

"So, madam," she greeted her with heavy irony, "you are come home at last! 'Tis no matter to you, I suppose, that work be left undone while you take yourself off to the village. It would have become you better to seek leave of me first."

Charity, her nerves tense from the emotions of the morning, felt her own temper rising, but forced it back. "I ask your pardon," she said mildly. "It would have been more courteous, I own, but the news of Darrell's return drove all else from my thoughts."

"I'll warrant it did," Mrs Shenfield agreed unpleasantly. " 'Twas ever thus, was it not? But mark this, my girl! Conduct permissible in a child—though even then, to my mind, you were allowed a deal too much licence—is not to be condoned in a grown woman. While you live in my house you will bear yourself modestly. There will be no more escapades like this morning's."

"That is unjust!" Charity's head came up; her voice was indignant. "To greet an old friend after long and perilous absence, to take to him the motherless son he had never seen—what immodesty lies in that?"

"In that, none, but do not suppose you can deceive me! You left the child at the inn and went off alone, and when you returned to the village, an hour and more later, Darrell Conyngton was with you. Do not seek to deny it!"

"I do not intend to!" Charity looked at her, and the contempt in her eyes brought the colour to Mrs Shenfield's face. "There is a spy in the village, it seems, nor does one need to look far in order to discover him. Dr Malperne displays a truly Christian spirit!"

"The Doctor is an honest and godly man, and evil-doing is an abomination in his eyes."

"As in the eyes of all God-fearing folk, aunt, but what virtue lies in seeing evil where none exists?"

Mrs Shenfield eyed her in a baffled way, for she could not in honesty convince herself that Charity's conduct that morning had been anything other than innocent, however irritating it might be. Finally she said sharply:

"Nor is he to be mocked at by a pert, irreverent girl! You would do well to pray for meekness, and for a proper deference towards those in authority over you. Yes, and for forgiveness for seeking to lead others into the paths of deceit! Your cousin Sarah sought this morning to conceal your absence from me."

"The blame for that is mine," Charity said quickly. "Pray do not punish her."

"Had I intended punishment it would already have been given, but I knew only too well where the true fault lay. Now get you gone, and see to it that all those tasks left undone this morning are completed before you sleep tonight."

"They shall be done," Charity replied quietly, "but first, madam, I am the bearer of a message from Darrell. He bade me tell you that he will come here later in the day to thank you and my uncle for the kindness you have used towards his son."

"We seek no thanks for an act of Christian charity," Mrs Shenfield said shortly. "It would be more to the point if he told us how soon we are to be rid of the burden."

"No doubt he will do so," Charity replied. "I know nothing of what he intends."

When Darrell arrived at the Moat House late that

afternoon he found the family assembled in the hall to greet him. All were conscious of the delicacy of the situation, and anxious that it should pass off with as little embarrassment as possible. Courteous greetings were exchanged, and Darrell looked with pity and dismay at Mr Shenfield. Charity had told him of her uncle's illness, but he was still profoundly shocked to find a man whom he remembered as hearty and robust so enfeebled.

Charity herself was aware of a vague uneasiness, nebulous as a gathering shadow. This meeting, though easy for none of them, must inevitably bear most heavily upon Darrell, and some signs of strain in him were natural enough. Yet she had the feeling that there was something more, some burden heavier even than the bitter thoughts and memories which, in this house above all others, must come crowding in upon him. Beneath the formal courtesy he seemed remote, withdrawn, different altogether from the man with whom she had talked that morning.

"I have come here," he said when they were all seated, "for two reasons. The first is to thank you, sir, and you also, Mrs Shenfield, for the kindness you showed my wife in her hour of need, and for the care you have given my son ever since his birth. For that I shall always be grateful to you."

"Grateful? To us?" Jonathan Shenfield smote his stick violently against the stone-flagged floor. His words, already marred by the paralysis which affected one side of his face, were rendered even more indistinct by sudden emotion, but their meaning was plain enough. "God's life, Sir Darrell! What cause have you for gratitude? We should be on our knees, begging forgiveness for the wrongs inflicted upon you by that cowardly renegade I am ashamed to call my son. His shame is ours, and must be for all time to come!"

This outburst smote them all into silence, for never before had Mr Shenfield betrayed the depths of his bitterness against Jonas. Elizabeth was the first to recover.

"We all regret what befell that day, but in time of war many deeds are done which would be unthinkable when the realm is at peace. Nothing is to be gained, husband, by reopening old wounds!"

"Nothing!" There was sudden weariness in Darrell's voice. "God knows that in the name of war I, too, have done deeds in which I take no pride. Let be, sir! The past is over and done!"

Charity stared at him, and the shadow of her uneasiness spread and darkened. This was not Darrell as she remembered him, this tired, defeated man who brushed aside in a few words the plundering and wanton destruction of his beautiful home, the loss of much of his land. Where now was the strong hand, the proud, unconquerable spirit, to which she and others like her had looked for guidance and protection?

"You spoke of two reasons for your visit, Sir Darrell," Mrs Shenfield said after a pause. "What may the second be?"

Darrell seemed to rouse himself with an effort from gloomy abstraction, and said quietly: "To seek a favour, madam, and beg that you will continue to shelter my son for a little while longer. It is scarcely possible for me to take him to the inn."

"Set your mind at rest, sir!" Elizabeth's words were more gracious than the tone in which they were uttered. "The child will naturally remain under our roof until you have reestablished your household."

"You mistake me, Mrs Shenfield." Darrell's voice was flat, as though he had deliberately excluded all expression from it. "I do not intend to remain in Conyngton St John. As soon as I have settled certain matters of business I return to Kent, and the boy with me. His grandmother, Lady Mordisford, is eager to have the care of him."

Charity, her face composed, her hands lightly clasped together in her lap, sat very still, wrapped in that numbness which is the first reaction to a mortal wound. Only her sudden pallor, her wide, stricken eyes, betrayed her, and Mrs Shenfield, casting one glance at her and another at Darrell's set face, summed up the situation swiftly and correctly. So the girl had not lied when she said she knew nothing of Conyngton's intentions.

"A wise and prudent decision, sir, I have no doubt," she said graciously. "It will be a comfort to Lady Mordisford to have her daughter's son to love and watch over. As for yourself, Sir Darrell, 'tis understandable that you should be reluctant to dwell again where so many painful memories abound."

No one paid any heed to her. Charity rose slowly to her feet and moved forward until she stood face to face with Darrell, who had also risen. She said in a whisper:

"You do not mean this?"

He bowed his head, as though he could not face the accusation in her eyes. "I should have told you this morning," he said in a low voice, "and for the fact that I did not I have no excuse save cowardice. Forgive me!"

For a few seconds longer she stood there, and then turned abruptly away. He tried to detain her, but she dashed his hand aside and fled along the hall to the stairs and went up them with stumbling haste. Mrs Shenfield said smoothly:

"Pray forgive this discourtesy, Sir Darrell! Charity is devoted to the child, but when she has grown accustomed to the thought of his departure she will realize that you are acting in his best interests."

Darrell gave no sign of having heard her. He stood, one hand gripping the back of the chair from which he had risen, and looked with troubled eyes towards the staircase where Charity had now passed out of sight. The taut silence was broken by Sarah's reproachful voice.

"How could you do that to her? How could you be so cruel?"

"Sarah, be silent!" Mrs Shenfield rebuked her in shocked tones, but her daughter was in no mood for obedience. She bounced up from her stool and confronted Darrell, her cheeks scarlet with anger and distress.

"I will not be silent! It will break Charity's heart to lose the child! Do you not realize, Sir Darrell, that she has lived only for him ever since the day of his birth? You are cruel, and ungrateful, and it would be better for all of us if you had never come back!"

She swung round with a swirl of petticoats and ran off in the direction her cousin had taken. Mrs Shenfield, outraged by such behaviour, made as though to fetch her back, but Darrell said quickly:

"No, let her go, and I pray you, madam, do not rebuke her for what she said. Never was accusation so well deserved!" He was silent for a moment, and then sighed and turned away. "I will take my leave now. My thanks again to you both for all that you have done."

He bowed abruptly and went quickly away. When the

sound of his footsteps had faded, Jonathan Shenfield raised his head and looked stonily at his wife.

"The proud Conyngtons humbled, and driven from the place that bears their name!" he said heavily. "You will have glad tidings, Elizabeth, to send to your son."

Mrs Shenfield paid no heed. In her mind she was already framing the sentences which she would presently write to Jonas, telling him of this final, unexpected defeat of the man whom they both looked upon as his enemy. She would warn Jonas not to return from Plymouth until Darrell had left Conyngton St John for good. Ever since the war ended it had been her constant nightmare that he would return and find some way of calling Jonas to account for the destruction of the manor, but now it seemed that his courage was lost along with all the rest. He would go, and take with him the child whose very existence, for some reason she could not even guess, seemed such an affront to her son whenever he came home.

So benevolent a mood did these reflections inspire in her that she made no attempt to punish Sarah for her impudence, or even to separate her from Charity for the rest of the evening. Charity, too, had been defeated that day. Elizabeth felt that those few moments in the hall had avenged her upon both the dark, defiant child she had never liked, and the woman whose demure, patient demeanour and scornful eyes so often roused her to baffled fury.

Sarah, following Charity to the nursery in a passion of loving sympathy, was disconcerted to find her playing with the little boy as though she had not just learned that he was to be wrested from her care and carried to the other side of England. She had come to comfort, and found herself staying to join their game, and if there was

155

a kind of desperation behind Charity's laughter and in her dark eyes it was a desperation which refused to be acknowledged.

Only that night, when all the rest of the house lay wrapped in sleep, did Charity at last give way to her despair. For years she had lived for the day just gone by, the day when Darrell would come home and she could share with him the burden of her hopes and fears. Now the day had come and gone, and she was left bereft and desolate, robbed even of hope. It was a stranger who had come back to Conyngton St John, and the moments of closeness that morning among the manor ruins a delusion like all the rest.

When the first grey pallor of dawn crept across the sky she rose and dressed. Little Darrell was still sleeping soundly in the narrow bed on the far side of the room, and for a few minutes she leaned lovingly over him, trying not to think of mornings when she would wake to find herself alone. A pain which was almost physical gripped her at the thought. She could not bring herself to face the prospect of parting with this child whom she loved so dearly for his own sweet sake, and more dearly still because he was Darrell's son.

She went softly from the room without rousing him, for Nurse was within earshot and would care for him when he awoke. Charity crept down the stairs, as she had done on so many other mornings during her life, and let herself out into the stableyard. The sun was rising, but a thick white mist, forerunner of heat to come, blanketed the countryside, and the grass in the park was still wet with dew.

She walked aimlessly, blind for once to the beauty about her, and found herself at last at the far edge of the woods, where the trees thinned and the gaunt ruins of Conyngton loomed through the dispersing mist. Gazing at the black skeleton of the great house, she reflected that it was small wonder Darrell shrank from living within sight of that bleak reminder of all he had lost. Yet even that thought held no consolation, for his decision to return to Kent had been no sudden impulse born of shock and grief. He had come home with no intention of remaining.

As she stood there at the edge of the woods, looking at the grim monument to her kinsman's hatred, she knew suddenly what she must do. The warning which yesterday compassion had urged her to withhold must be spoken now, and Darrell made aware of Jonas's intentions. She straightened her shoulders, and, resolute now, walked briskly across the park towards the village.

At the inn Abigail greeted her with astonishment, and the information that Sir Darrell had not yet risen. She looked with concern at the girl's drawn face and shadowed eyes and inquired anxiously whether anything were amiss with the little master.

"No, nothing at all," Charity said wearily. "Abigail, will you have Diccon or Peter rouse Sir Darrell and tell him that I am here? It is necessary that I speak with him, but I must be back at the Moat House before my aunt learns of my absence. I will wait by the river."

She went out again before Abigail could protest, and walked past the bowling green to the river bank, where, in a secluded spot among the trees, she sat down to wait for Darrell. The sun had cleared the mist by now, and the sparkle of it on the water rippling past a few yards away dazzled her. She rested her head against the trunk of the tree behind her and closed her eyes, and after a minute or two the warmth of the sun and the soft chuckle of the river lulled her into a doze. She awoke with a start at the sound of her name, to find Darrell on one knee beside her, regarding her with an expression half amused and half concerned. He looked so much like the Darrell she had always known that the considered phrases rehearsed on the way to the village were quite forgotten, and she said with simple entreaty:

"Darrell, I beg of you, do not leave us again!"

She saw his expression change and harden, the affectionate amusement fade from his eyes. He rose abruptly to his feet, saying in a cold voice: "Did you come here with such urgency and have me haled from bed merely to ask me that?"

Charity got up also. Weariness, and the sudden waking, made her feel dizzy, and she leaned one hand against the tree to steady herself.

"Is it so small a thing? Darrell, you do not know! You think that Jonas's hatred is satisfied, but it is not, nor will be while you still possess one cottage or one acre of land. Nothing less than your utter ruin will satisfy him. I know, for he has told me so."

He shrugged. "Then let him but have patience! Time, and his victorious leaders at Westminster, will accomplish it for him."

"He wants more than that! Your ruin, yes, but what you lose he means to possess. Already he has begun to buy your land, and I'll warrant that if ever he feels an instant's remorse for the burning of Conyngton 'tis because it placed *that* beyond his reach for all time. He sees himself as squire of Conyngton St John."

He regarded her with sombre eyes. "And you would have me bide here to see it also?"

"I would have you stay to prevent it, for your son's

158

sake if you will not for your own! In the name of God, Darrell, what ails you that you grow so laggard in guarding what is yours?"

"I will tell you what ails me!" Sudden anger throbbed in his voice and drove the indifference from his eyes. "Four years of war and fighting and fruitless slaughter! My father at Edgehill, my cousin Nicholas at Newbury, kinsmen, friends, and servants upon a dozen battlefields throughout the length and breadth of England. And for what? The King is a prisoner, and the cause we fought for defeated! Here in Devon my wife and mother also lie dead, my home is in ruins and my fortune gone."

"And your courage also, it seems!" Out of bitter disappointment her temper flared to match his own. "Are you the only one to have suffered? There is scarcely a house in this parish—in all England, for that matter—that has not known sorrow and loss these past few years! Scarcely a living soul who does not mourn someone dear to them! Yet sacrifice is only in vain if those who remain allow it to be so."

"You are full of wisdom and brave counsel, are you not?" he retorted bitterly. "But words alone accomplish nothing. Yesterday your aunt spoke glibly to me of re-establishing my household. Where, in God's name, and with what? There is no money left with which to rebuild Conyngton."

"You still have the Dower House!"

"The Dower House?" For an instant there was an arrested expression in his eyes, but then he shook his head. " 'Twould not be fit to live in. It has stood empty for years."

She shook her head. "For little more than three. Mr Partridge dwelt there until his death, with those of the servants who had not fled or returned to their homes, and before that it was always well cared for. It would not be so great a task to set it to rights." She laid her hand on his arm, and from angry her voice became pleading. "Darrell, I entreat you to remain here! What if your lands *are* less broad than once they were? Those which remain are still the equal of many an estate, and could be made prosperous again. Every man and woman dwelling upon them would gladly work until they drop for you and for your son, and in return ask only that you should be their guide and protector as the squire has always been. Where else can they look for help if not to you?"

She paused, looking anxiously at him, but he made no response. He had turned his head away and was staring past her at the sunlit river, his expression bleak and unrelenting. Her heart sank, but she would not so easily admit defeat.

"If you leave the heart will go out of this village, and its people fall a ready prey to Jonas and his henchman Dr Malperne. These are *your* people, Darrell! They have waited and prayed for your return and you cannot turn your back upon them now. I do not pretend that it will be easy! There will be many difficulties to overcome, but——"

"In the fiend's name, Charity, will you be silent!" he broke in, rounding upon her with such fury that she recoiled. "I have had a surfeit of your reproaches this day, and though I own I was at fault in not confiding my intentions to you at the outset, that gives you no right to tell me what I should or should not do. The simple truth is that I no longer desire to live in Conyngton St John! Now plague me no more!"

She had been about to tell him of the jewels hidden in

the tower by the moat, hoping that the disclosure might make the difficulties confronting him seem less insurmountable, but his unexpected attack drove all thought of them from her mind. For a moment she was too astonished to speak, and could only stare blankly at him. Then slowly amazement gave way to anger again, and to a bitter contempt which she did not trouble to conceal.

"You no longer desire to live in Conyngton St John," she repeated in a low, furious voice, "and so you will take your son and go! You do not pause to reflect that there may be others equally loth to dwell here, but who lack your good fortune in having the means to depart. People who, for love of you, have not hesitated to show Jonas how they hate and despise him, and who will therefore suffer most at his hands when he is master here, as he will be if you neglect your duty towards them now. God's mercy! Are five years enough to destroy all ties of affection, all duty towards what you were taught to regard as a sacred trust?"

A flush, partly of anger and partly of shame, darkened his cheeks as she spoke, and when she paused he said quickly: "I am not lost to all sense of gratitude, Charity, and it was never my intention that *you* should be left to bear the brunt of your kinsman's malice. I know how dearly you love the child, and how he clings to you, and when I return to Kent I want you to come with me."

"To come . . . ?" Charity was once again almost bereft of words. "As little Darrell's nurse? You imagine that would be permitted?"

"No," he said angrily, "nor would I have the insolence to suggest it. I want you to come as my wife!"

5

The Ultimate Loyalty

It seemed to Charity that a curious stillness followed his words, as though the whole world had been stunned into silence, and in the stillness someone was laughing. It was a second or two before she realized that it was herself.

"I am gratified, madam, that you are amused," Darrell said icily. The colour had receded from his face, leaving it white and set with anger. "I did not, however, speak in jest."

"Forgive me! That was unmannerly!" she replied unsteadily. She could not tell him that she laughed at the tragic irony of it, this talk of marriage in the midst of the first bitter quarrel they had ever had, this unlooked-for flowering of his dead mother's secret, hopeless wish. "But you must surely know that such a thing is even less likely to be permitted than that I should come as your servant."

He frowned. "I do not know it! To be sure, I am no

longer a rich man, but I am still far from being a pauper, while you——"

"While I am nothing but a penniless orphan, as Jonas never tires of reminding me," she interrupted him. "Do you not see that for this reason alone I would never be permitted to marry you? My aunt Elizabeth would die rather than see *me* become 'my lady'."

"The decision will not rest with her, nor yet with Jonas. Your uncle is your guardian, and though his health may be enfeebled, his wits are not, and I do not believe that he will withhold his consent."

Charity turned abruptly away and stood with bowed head, in the grip of a temptation so sudden and so strong that it seemed she must succumb to it. What Darrell said was true, and she knew that if she now behaved meekly and dutifully there need be no parting from the two people she loved best in the world: Darrell himself, and the child whom she had cherished from the day of his birth. A woman had few rights. Unquestioning obedience, first to her father or guardian, and later to her husband, was demanded of her. No one would blame her now if she passively allowed her future to be settled for her by Darrell and her uncle.

No one? Charity looked across the river at the mill, and the tower of the church rising among the trees beyond, which was all that could be seen of the village from where she stood, and thought of the loyal and trusting folk who dwelt there. Folk who had fought and sacrificed and suffered for the Royal cause, not because they knew the rights and wrongs of the quarrel between King and Parliament but because the Conyngtons had told them it was their duty to do so; who had regarded the victorious Roundheads with silent hostility, and waited patiently for the squire to return, assuring one another that all would be well once they had a Conyngton to guide and help them once more. She knew without vanity that they would be glad to see her become the squire's lady, and that because they loved both her and Darrell they might even forgive them for abandoning the village. But she knew that she would never forgive herself.

"Darrell!" She turned towards him again, her low voice unsteady with the intensity of her pleading. "You told me once that though you would fight for Church and King, 'twas here that your ultimate loyalty lay. I entreat you, do not forswear that loyalty now! It is needed as never before! If you wish me to be your wife I will gladly wed you, and strive by God's grace to lighten your labours and your sorrows, but not if I must leave this place we both love so well."

"Do not try to bargain with me, Charity," he said coldly. "My decision was made long before I returned, but do not think it was lightly or easily taken. One thing only lured me back—the thought of my son, and of you—but it was to take you both hence that I came, and not to be persuaded into staying."

"For your son, Darrell, you have every right to decide," she replied quietly, "but not for me."

"I think I have. You have long been as close to me as any sister, and when you came to live at Conyngton the responsibility for your future became mine. That alone gives me the right you speak of, even without the immeasurable debt I owe you."

"Yet you will not stay in Conyngton St John?"

He shook his head. "I will not stay."

"Then I cannot marry you," she said with a sigh, "for I

will not go. You have made your decision, Darrell, and I mine."

"Stubborn as ever, are you not?" he said impatiently. "What in God's name do you think to accomplish by remaining here?"

"Nothing," she said sadly, "for even now I am of little account at the Moat House, and when my uncle dies I shall be even less. Yet stay I must, for conscience' sake! I have friends here, and know where my duty lies."

"And I do not!" he retorted angrily. "Is that what you would say?"

"I think you know well enough, Darrell, but you will not own it."

"Yes, Madam Impertinence, I know it! My first duty is to my son, and after that to you, without whose care my son could never have survived."

"No," she said bitterly, "you owe *me* no duty! What I did for the child was done out of tenderness for him, and out of the love and gratitude I bear towards all your family. Aye, and because I made a promise, years agone! There is no debt betwixt you and me—certainly not one so great that you are obliged to offer me marriage in settlement of it."

"That was not my meaning! Deliberately you twist my words into weapons against me."

"Words!" she repeated, her temper beginning to rise again. " 'Tis by our deeds that we are judged, and if you now desert those who depend upon you, then by that deed will you stand condemned. Before God, I believe Darrell Conyngton must, after all, have perished in the wars, for he whom I once knew by that name would never have sought so diligently to evade his clear duty!"

"Do you call me 'coward'?" His voice was low and

furious, and he seized her by the shoulders in a grip that made her gasp. "By God, Charity, I'll not take that, even from you!"

"Not 'coward'," she retorted, her gaze meeting his defiantly. "For cowardice you might be pitied, even forgiven. No, 'tis pride that drives you hence, a warped and twisted pride with nothing of honour in it. Your great house gone, your fortune drained away, your lands diminished—that is what *you* cannot face, Darrell! That is why you are ready to betray your trust, your duty, the very name you bear! Now loose me, and let me go! We have no more to say to one another."

For a moment or two he continued to hold her, but then before her challenging regard his own gaze faltered and turned away. His hands dropped from her shoulders, and she stepped past him and went towards the inn without a backward glance.

She did not enter the house, but passed behind it by way of a path which brought her after a minute or two to the road she had taken the previous morning when she went to seek Darrell at Conyngton. Then she had walked eagerly, light of heart and foot, but now disappointment and sorrow lay like a heavy burden upon her. She went wearily up the hill, and though she passed within a few hundred yards of the burned-out manor, did not even glance in that direction. Now something even more precious had been destroyed. A house might some day be rebuilt, but who could repair a broken trust, a loved ideal shattered and dishonoured?

It was not until the following day that the thought of the jewels once more occurred to her. She remembered them with dismay, for she had resolved, in the grief and disillusion of the previous day, never to see Darrell again. Everything had been said that morning by the river. To see him again would only increase intolerably her disappointment and anger, and the hurt which was harder to bear than either.

Yet now it seemed that meet again they must. There was no question of not returning the jewels, for, whatever use he chose to make of them, they were Darrell's property, a legacy from his wife and his mother, and no one else had a shadow of right to them. That night, when the rest of the household was sleeping, she retrieved the casket from its hiding-place in the tower and concealed it instead on a ledge high up within the nursery fireplace. There it could lie unsuspected until an opportunity occurred to restore it to Darrell.

The problem of how best to accomplish this occupied her mind during the earlier part of the following day, until it was driven thence by an occurrence which cast the whole household into a state of apprehension and dismay. Charity was in the nursery, busy at the spinning-wheel while little Darrell struggled with his lessons, when Sarah burst into the room, her face white and terrified.

"Charity!" she gasped. "Oh, Charity, my father's sickness has stricken him again, more dreadfully than before! He can neither speak nor move!"

The spinning-wheel slowed and stopped as Charity stared in consternation at her cousin. Sarah went on distractedly:

"I went to the parlour to read to him, as I always do at this hour, and found that he had fallen from his chair and was lying on the floor. Oh, Charity, I thought he was dead!"

She burst into tears and buried her face in her hands, and Charity jumped up and went quickly to take her in her arms. At the table, little Darrell began to whimper also, uncomprehending but alarmed.

"Hush, Sarah dear! You are frightening the child!" Charity's voice was steady, belying the feeling of sick dismay that clutched at her stomach. "Where is my uncle now?"

"I ran to fetch Mother, and she summoned the servants to carry him to his bedchamber!" Sarah was making a valiant effort to control her voice. "I should have stayed with her, but, God forgive me, I was too frightened!"

"I will go to my aunt," Charity said in a low voice. "Do you stay here, Sarah, and try to reassure the child."

When she reached her uncle's room she found Nurse and one or two of the upper servants there before her. It was plain that everything possible had already been done to restore him, but in vain. He lay motionless and corpse-like in the big bed, with only his scarcely perceptible breathing to show that he still lived. Mrs Shenfield, who was standing beside the bed, looked round at her niece as the girl came to join her and said in a low voice:

"Go to the stables, Charity, and bid William ride at once to summon Jonas from Plymouth. Tell him to make all haste he can."

Jonas arrived at the Moat House late that night, bringing a physician with him, but the doctor was able to hold out little hope of Mr Shenfield's recovery, or indeed of any improvement in his condition. The following day he returned to Plymouth, but Jonas remained at the Moat House, sending William off again, this time to bear an urgent summons to Beth at her husband's house near Exeter.

Charity, taking her share of duties in the sick-room, thought pityingly that death could come only as a mercy,

168

a welcome release from the living death to which her uncle was now condemned. He remained utterly helpless, too helpless even to give his blessing to his son and daughters when they gathered at his bedside, and though Jonas wore a grave and melancholy air, and spent much time in prayer, this did not deter him from taking upon himself that part of his father's authority which had hitherto been denied him. He was master of the Moat House now in all but name, and could not wholly conceal the satisfaction this gave him.

Charity had now no leisure for her own affairs; scarcely, indeed, for any thought not immediately concerned with domestic tasks. Ever since her enforced return to the Moat House her aunt had worked her hard, and now, in addition to her usual duties, and the care of the little boy, there was the sick man to be tended also. She knew that more than her fair share of these labours was being thrust upon her, but she welcomed the work which kept her occupied from dawn till dark and left her so weary that she fell asleep as soon as she laid her head upon the pillow. Thus, at least, she was spared the pain and futility of dwelling upon what had passed, and of contemplating the emptiness which would encompass her life when the child was taken from her.

So the long, summer days slipped by almost unnoticed, lengthening into weeks, while Jonathan Shenfield's spirit still lingered in the prison of his helpless body. Darrell did not come again to the Moat House—while Jonas was there it was scarcely to be expected that he would—and Charity, hearing no news of him, concluded that he was still occupied with the business of which he had spoken, and which she supposed to be concerned with the future of the remaining Conyngton lands. Each day she dreaded to see him, for when he came it would be to take away his son.

On a hot, still August afternoon she was walking with the little boy beside the moat. She had taken him to their favourite retreat beneath the willow tree, with the intention of pursuing his neglected lessons, but so tired was she—for she had lately been keeping old Nurse's nocturnal vigils in the sick-room as well as her own—that she had found herself falling repeatedly into a doze. With the broad, deep pool so close at hand this negligence was dangerous to the child, and she had felt obliged to return to the house.

Darrell had pouted a little at this, but walked beside her obediently enough until they reached the other end of the moat, where the track leading across the park to the road passed close to the pool. Then he flung out a pointing hand.

"Look! Look!" he exclaimed excitedly. "Someone is coming! Perhaps it is my father!"

Charity's heart lurched with mingled hope and dismay as she followed the direction of the pointing finger, but she saw at once that the man riding towards them was not Darrell. He was a stranger to her, and since he was dressed in the gay clothes and plumed hat of the Cavalier she paused to watch his approach, wondering who he might be, and what errand brought him to the Moat House. As he drew nearer she saw that he was young, with a handsome, rather delicately featured face and curling, light brown hair.

He reined in his horse when he reached them and sat staring at the little boy, who returned the look with one of doubtful curiosity, pressing himself close to Charity's side. She put her arm round him in an unconsciously protective

170

gesture, for there was a curious expression in the stranger's face.

"No need, my child, to ask whose son *you* are," he said in a low voice after a moment. Then for the first time he looked directly at Charity, and she had the immediate impression that though she did not know him, his face was not altogether unfamiliar. "And I doubt not, madam, that you are Miss Shenfield?"

She nodded, more puzzled than ever. "I am Charity Shenfield, but I think, sir, that I do not know you."

"Forgive me!" He came swiftly down from the saddle and swept off his hat to make her a low bow. "Permit me to present myself. I am Henry Mordisford."

"Mordisford!" she repeated, realizing now why those dark grey eyes struck such a chord of memory. "Then you are Alison's kinsman?"

"Her youngest brother, madam, and therefore uncle to this imp who bears her likeness in his face." He looked again at the child, smiling and holding out an inviting hand. "Well, nephew? I have journeyed a great way to make your acquaintance."

Darrell hung back, leaning still closer to Charity and casting an anxious, questioning glance up at her. She said apologetically to Mordisford:

"I fear he is shy, sir, and unused to strangers."

"Another legacy from his mother," Henry Mordisford said ruefully. "Poor Alison! No creature more shy than she ever walked this earth." He tweaked gently at a strand of silky hair which strayed across the child's forehead. "Have you no more of your father about you, boy, than his name and his russet hair?"

Charity watched him uneasily, for now that her first surprise was fading she saw in this pleasant young man merely another harbinger of her own future loneliness and sorrow. A little chill seemed to touch her, even in the heat of the day, and she said in a breathless, unsteady voice:

"Do you come from Sir Darrell, Mr Mordisford?"

He shook his head. "No, Miss Shenfield, I arrived in Conyngton St John only an hour or two agone. I sought in vain for Sir Darrell, and then resolved to come in search of you and my nephew without delay. It was in my mind that I might learn from you where Sir Darrell may be found."

"I have not seen Sir Darrell, sir, since the day after he came home," she replied with as much composure as she could command. "My uncle fell grievously sick about that time, and I have now no leisure to go abroad."

"I am sorry to hear it, madam!" Mordisford's tone was puzzled. "Yet Sir Darrell comes here, surely, to see his son?"

Charity shook her head, meeting his eyes steadily with her own direct gaze. "I do not know, Mr Mordisford, how fully you are informed upon matters in Conyngton St John but you must at least be aware that it was my cousin Jonas who led the Roundheads here on the day the manor was destroyed. Jonas has been at the Moat House ever since his father was stricken, and so it is not to be marvelled at that Darrell comes not here."

She paused, as from the garden beyond the ancient wall came the sound of Sarah's voice speaking to one of the servants. Charity bent towards little Darrell and said quickly:

"My dear one, Sarah is yonder in the garden. Run to her, and bid her come hither to me." He trotted off obediently, and she straightened up again and looked at Henry Mordisford. "There is a favour, sir, which I must ask of

172

you, and of which I could not speak before the child. He does not yet know that he is to be taken from my care, nor would it be any kindness to tell him before 'tis needful. When the time comes I will make him understand that it is best for him."

She broke off, realizing that her companion was looking at her in astonishment, and after a moment he said incredulously:

"Miss Shenfield, is it possible that you, of all people, do not know; that Darrell has not yet told you——"

"Told me what, sir?" She heard her own voice sharp with sudden urgency. "I do not understand!"

"Why, that he no longer intends to leave Conyngton St John! That he is already living at the Dower House, and from all accounts is determined to remain there."

Charity stared at him, torn between disbelief, astonishment, and the beginnings of great gladness. She said in a whisper: "Sir, are you sure of this?"

"Most certainly I am. When Darrell left our home in June it was with every intention of returning, but when at last news came from him it was that which my mother, at least, had no desire to receive. His letter informed us that he had been brought to realize that, no matter how changed his fortunes, his place was here." He paused, looking quizzically at her as though he suspected that she might have had some influence upon that decision, but when she did not speak, he went on: "Therefore I came—no, let us say, rather, I was sent—to discover what had prompted the resolve, and to seek, if possible, to change it."

"Mr Mordisford!" Charity's voice was low, and charged with a desperate earnestness. "If Darrell now means to stay do not, I beg of you, try to shake his

173

resolve. He is needed here—you cannot know how much."

He laughed. "Madam, I said I was sent for that purpose, not that I had any intention of fulfilling it. To my mind, Darrell was over-persuaded into his first decision, for my mother is urgent in her wish to have Alison's son in her own charge." He hesitated for a moment, and when he spoke again there was no longer any levity in his voice. "Darrell Conyngton is my friend. We fought together, and together saw our cause go down in ruin and defeat, but when all was done *I* still had my home to which to return, my family awaiting me. There is no need to tell *you* how much greater Darrell's losses were than mine! He came with me to Kent, embittered and lonely, and it was not difficult for my mother to convince him that nothing mattered now except the child, and that the child's place was with her. I doubted then the wisdom of such a course, and now that Darrell's own choice proves me right, rest assured that I shall not seek to change his mind."

"I thank you, sir," she replied unsteadily. "You may think, perhaps, that my desire for him to stay springs but from selfishness, but, believe me, that is not entirely so. There are reasons——"

She broke off, suddenly aware that Henry Mordisford's attention was no longer upon her. He was looking past her towards the garden, and when Charity turned she saw that the child was coming back to them, leading Sarah by the hand. The strain of the past weeks had told upon Sarah as upon everyone at the Moat House. Her face had lost something of its childish roundness and her usual bubbling merriment was subdued, and yet in some subtle way she looked prettier than ever before. As she came up to them, Charity said in greeting:

"Sarah, we have a guest—little Darrell's uncle, Mr Mordisford. Sir, this is my cousin, Sarah Shenfield."

Sarah curtsied, Henry Mordisford bowed, and then they stood gazing at each other without speaking. Colour had risen rosily in the girl's face, the young man had lost a little of his earlier assurance, and as Charity looked from one to the other she realized that for both of them she, the child, their very surroundings, had ceased to exist. Dismay swept over her, for of what use was it for Puritan maid and Cavalier to look at each other with such rapture in their eyes?

6

At the Dower House

Whatever emotion, however, had sprung into being between Sarah Shenfield and Henry Mordisford in that first moment of meeting it did not dominate Charity's thoughts for long. Her mind was too ful of the news Mordisford had brought. Until now the thought of the future had been a threat hanging over her, a dread she had been almost afraid to acknowledge. If Darrell had left Conyngton St John for good, and Sarah presently married, as she was bound to do, she would have been left utterly friendless, compelled to live in a house where she was neither liked nor wanted, obliged to work with the servants and yet prevented, by her close kinship with the family, from finding any real place among them. Now, at last, the threat had been lifted.

It was only later, when during the evening she was taking her turn in the sick-room, that full realization came of the cruel trick fortune had played upon her. Had she been less adamant in her refusal to leave the village she might have been promised to Darrell before her uncle's mortal sickness struck him, and once they had plighted troth even Jonas would have found it difficult to prevent their marriage. There could be no hope of such a marriage now, even if Darrell still desired it. For all practical purposes Jonas was already her guardian, and to him it was as natural as breathing to thwart Darrell in every conceivable way. Charity could imagine with what glee he would seize upon this opportunity.

She felt certain now that Jonas had known, or at least suspected, Darrell's decision, and deliberately concealed it from her, for he had shown little surprise at Henry Mordisford's news. Charity knew that Dr Malperne kept him informed of all that went on in the village, and he must already have seen, in Darrell's occupation of the Dower House, a threat to his own schemes. It was typical of him to wrest what satisfaction he could from the event by keeping her in ignorance of it.

Mr Mordisford had stayed only a brief time at the Moat House, but before departing he had sought leave to come again on the morrow to see his nephew. Charity thought it more likely that his purpose was to see Sarah, for though by the time they entered the house he was sufficiently in command of himself to dissemble his earlier bedazzlement, he could not resist the temptation to glance frequently in her direction. Sarah herself, younger and less worldly than he, found it more difficult to hide her feelings, hanging breathlessly upon his words and blushing hotly whenever she chanced to meet his eyes. Charity could only hope that her behaviour had escaped the notice of Jonas and his mother.

Her own most urgent desire now was to see Darrell

again, and to make amends, if possible, for the hard things she had said to him, but she knew that if she went to the Dower House it would have to be by night. Every hour of her day was so filled with tasks of one sort and another that it would be impossible to slip away undetected. Secrecy was of prime importance, the more so since she intended to take the Conyngton jewels with her. The sooner they were safely in Darrell's possession now, the better it would be.

It was Elizabeth's turn to sit up with Mr Shenfield during the latter part of the night, and when at about midnight she came to take her niece's place, the rest of the household were already in bed and asleep. Charity went softly through the silent house to the nursery, where, first assuring herself that the little boy was sleeping soundly, she fetched the jewel-box from its hiding-place. Then, casting a light cloak about her to conceal her burden, she crept down the back stairs and out by way of the stableyard. A dog stirred, and growled deep in its throat, but she whispered to it to be still and at the sound of a familiar voice it subsided again with a faint rattle of its chain.

Darkness had brought little relief from the heat of the day. The air was close and sultry, and though a crescent moon rode the sky, dark banks of cloud were piling up over Dartmoor. By the time Charity had completed the arduous climb through the woods she was hot and breathless, and paused to rest for a minute before going on. The snap of a twig and a faint rustling in the undergrowth on the slope below her made her jump, and then she relaxed again with a smile at her own foolishness as some small creature scurried past her and out of sight.

She moved away from the shadow of the woods and

started across the park towards the Dower House. She knew that when she got there she would have to rouse the household, but whatever servants Darrell employed would be Conyngton folk and she need fear no betrayal from them.

When she reached the house, however, and passed through the belt of trees surrounding the garden, she saw to her surprise that a light was burning in one of the lower rooms, where a casement stood wide to the summer night. She went cautiously forward and stood on tiptoe to look within.

A cluster of candles on the table in its centre made an island of brightness in the shadows of the big, panelled room. The table itself was littered with papers, and in the chair at its head, facing the window, Darrell was sitting. Ink and quill were on the table before him, but his hands lay idle on the arms of the chair, his head rested against the high, carved back, and his eyes were closed. There was such weariness in his face that Charity was conscious of a sudden, overwhelming tenderness, and a deeper understanding of what it had cost him to make the decision to remain at his stricken home. She lifted her hand and tapped softly against the casement.

With a start he opened his eyes and looked about him in bewilderment, then, as she tapped again, thrust back his chair and came quickly towards the window. She said in a whisper:

"Darrell, 'tis I—Charity!"

"Charity?" he repeated blankly. "What in the name of heaven brings you here at this hour?" Then, in sudden, swift anxiety: "The child . . . ?"

"No! No, all is well, but I must speak to you. Will you let me in?"

For a moment he looked down at her, frowning, and then signed abruptly to her to go to the door. He had it open by the time she reached it and she stepped into the house, but neither spoke until they were in the room he had just left, and the door closed behind them. Darrell set the candles down again on the table, but before he could speak, Charity, still clutching her burden to her beneath the cloak, said urgently:

"Pray close the window, Darrell, and the curtains also. I doubt there is none to spy upon us, but what I have to tell you is best close-guarded."

He looked surprised, but went to do as she asked. When he turned to face her again she flung off her cloak and laid the box on the table.

"Your mother's jewels, Darrell, and Alison's," she said simply. "They were left in my care. Here is the key."

She took it from her pocket and held it out to him, but at first he made no move to take it. Looking incredulously from her to the box and back again, he said slowly:

"I do not understand. The jewels were lost with all the rest when the Roundheads plundered Conyngton."

She shook her head. "It was to prevent such a misfortune that Lady Conyngton had me hide them. Everyone save Mr Partridge believed that they had been sold to raise money for the King."

Briefly she told him of the night when she had concealed the jewels, and how until a few weeks ago they had lain hidden in the tower. "I should have told you of them when you first returned," she concluded in a low voice, "but after my uncle fell ill there was no opportunity. Pray believe, though, that I would have found some means of conveying them to you before you left Devonshire."

She held out the key again and this time he came towards her, but instead of taking it, enfolded the hand which held it in both his own, looking at her with the glimmer of a smile.

"Do you imagine I could suppose for one instant that you would not?" he said gently. "My dear little sister, I know you too well for that."

She looked up at him, her dark eyes grave and troubled. "I would not have sought to rob you of the jewels," she replied unsteadily, "but my conscience is heavily burdened none the less, for I cannot forget the hard, cruel things I said to you that day by the river. Darrell, can you forgive me for that?"

"Forgive you for showing me the truth?" he said ruefully. "It would be more fitting if I thanked you for it! Oh, I will not deny I was angry!" A fleeting smile touched his lips again. "More angry with you than I had ever been in my life. But later, when my temper had cooled, I realized the justice of what you said. I think I had known it all the while, but had no wish to be confronted with the unflattering mirror you held up to me."

"I had no notion that you meant to stay here after all," she said slowly. "Each day I have dreaded to hear that you were ready to depart."

"I would have come to tell you, but then your uncle fell ill again and Jonas came home, and him I could not trust myself to face. I knew that when you learned that I had come here, to the Dower House, you would realize it it was my intention to remain."

Charity looked around her. The Dower House had been built at the same time as the manor and in the same style, though on a much smaller scale. The room in which they stood was oak-panelled from floor to moulded ceiling, the furniture heavy and handsome, the fireplace a vast cavern flanked by stone pillars elaborately carved. Yet even by candlelight the window-hangings and the cushions on the day-bed near the hearth showed faded and moth-eaten, and there still hung about it the all-pervading, musty atmosphere of a house which had long stood empty and untended. Darrell followed the direction of her glance and frowned.

" 'Tis scarcely home-like at present," he admitted, "but no doubt I should be grateful to have a roof still over my head, a house, however neglected, to call my own. Had Jonas turned aside to destroy this also I should be in parlous plight indeed."

"This is a pleasant house," Charity said stoutly. "Not grand or beautiful in the way that Conyngton was, but when 'tis cared for it can be a pleasant and comfortable home. You will see!"

"At present I can do no more than make it habitable. There is little enough gold to spare, and what I have must go where it is most urgently needed—into the land, which is the only real wealth." He gestured towards the papers littering the table, adding with a rueful laugh: "Each night I sit here, pondering ways and means, seeking to make each gold piece do the work of two, and wishing that I had poor Nick Hallett, or old Partridge, to give me aid. Four years of soldiering have left me unfitted for more peaceful business."

"You will contrive," she said with a smile, "and these will make your task easier, will they not?"

She turned to the table and fitted the key into the lock of the box she had placed there. At first, stiff and rusty, it resisted her efforts to turn it, but she succeeded at last and lifted the lid. The gleam of gold and the glitter of jewels, a little dulled now, shimmered in the candlelight, and Darrell and Charity stood side by side, looking down at them.

"It is your mother's legacy to you, Darrell," Charity said softly at length. " 'Twas only a week before she died that she called Alison and me to her and told us we must hide the jewels. Not one of us guessed then how wise and momentous her decision was to prove."

Darrell did not reply, scarcely seemed even to have heard what she said. He stretched out his hand and took from the box the beautiful string of pearls which he had given to Alison as a wedding-gift, and which she had worn constantly during their brief married life. Holding it gently between his hands, he stood looking down at it with infinite sadness in his face, and suddenly and without warning Charity found herself shaken by emotions so violent that they frightened her. She turned abruptly away, appalled at the intensity of her own feelings, at the knowledge that she could feel this fierce, implacable jealousy of a woman four years dead, a woman who had been her friend. Hardly aware of what she did, she moved across to the day-bed and sat down, leaning forward with her elbows on her knees and her face hidden in her hands.

"Charity!" Darrell's voice was startled, sharp with concern. "What is it? Are you ill?"

He dropped the pearls back into the box and came towards her, and she raised her head, forcing herself to face him calmly. "No, I am tired, nothing more! I have been up these four nights past, tending my uncle."

He seated himself beside her, looking at her so searchingly that she felt unable to sustain his regard, and turned her head away.

"It is my belief that they work you too hard at the Moat House," he said angrily, "and lay upon your shoulders burdens too heavy for them to bear." He reached out to clasp her lightly by the wrist. "Why, you are worn almost to a shadow."

She shook her head, forcing a smile and trying to ignore the touch of his fingers which was like fire against her skin. "You know that I have always been thin, and as for the work I do—well, Nurse should have kept vigil two nights out of the four, but she grows old and feeble and finds this hot weather sadly wearisome. Let me be, Darrell! I am well enough."

Reluctantly he slackened his hold, and she withdrew her hand and got up. That she was tired was true enough, but she was also frightened and bewildered by the storm of conflicting feelings which had suddenly taken possession of her, and her instinctive desire was to retreat. There was danger of self-betrayal in every moment that she lingered.

"I must go," she said distractedly. "It would go hard with me if my aunt or Jonas discovered I had been here. Bestow the jewels in some safe place, Darrell, for no living soul save you and I yet knows that they are still in your possession."

"Charity, wait!" Darrell had also risen, and now put out a hand to detain her. "There is much still to be said, and with Jonas at the Moat House I cannot tell when another opportunity to speak may offer itself." She made a little gesture of protest, guessing what he was about to say, but he paid no heed. "When last we talked together," he went on, "I asked you to be my wife, and you refused because I said I would not stay in Conyngton St John.

184

You know now that I do intend to stay. Will you give me a different answer tonight?"

She shook her head, not looking at him. "What use to speak of this? We both know it would never be permitted."

"That is not what I asked. At this moment I am concerned only to know whether you would be willing to marry me."

She made no reply, and after a moment he added quietly: "I need you, Charity, and so does the child. Do you not think we might find a measure of contentment together?"

Charity turned sharply away and stood gripping the high, carved back of a chair, trying to control a sudden trembling, the heavy, breathless pounding of her heart. "I need you," he had said, but that was not what she longed to hear, nor was it mere contentment she wanted to share with him. He looked upon her still as a sister, but for her the old, easy comradeship had gone for ever. This night had taught her that she loved him as a woman loves a man, and that with all the strength of her intense and passionate nature. Yet he was haunted still by the memory of his lost and lovely bride, and how could she prevail against that fair ghost, or hope to win his heart while his dead love looked at him from the face of their little son?

"It would not be permitted," she said again in a lifeless voice. "I think you do not realize, Darrell, how matters now stand at the Moat House. My poor uncle suffers a death-in-life, and Jonas fills his place as my guardian. I do not need to tell you that *he* would never consent to our marriage, and if he knew that you desired it he would never cease to taunt us. Do not, I beg of you, give him this added reason to flout you. Let us agree never to speak of this matter again."

She paused, but he did not reply and she could not find the courage to turn and look at him. Gripping harder than ever on the back of the chair, dimly aware of hurt as the ornately carved wood bit into her palms, she went on in the same dead tone:

"That you feel the need to wed again I understand, but there must be many women more fitted than I to be your wife, and if you choose wisely little Darrell will learn to love his step-mother as dearly as he now loves me."

"So many words, and my question still unanswered!" Darrell had moved closer to her and now his hands on her shoulders were turning her gently to face him. "Little one, of what are you afraid?"

She tried to break from his hold, pressing one hand to her forehead. The room seemed suddenly unbearably hot and airless, and a savage pain had begun to pound behind her eyes, so that even the feeble light of the guttering candles seemed intolerably bright. She tried to say again that she must go, but her tongue refused to frame the words, and then there was a brief period of blankness from which she emerged after a minute or so to find herself lying among the cushions on the day-bed with Darrell bending anxiously over her. He had flung back the curtains and opened the window wide once more, and though the night was sultry and thunderous a faint current of air was stealing into the room. Charity looked incredulously up at him.

"Did I swoon?" He nodded, and she went on disgustedly: "Why, what folly! I have never done so in my life! Forgive me, Darrell!"

"That is folly indeed, to ask forgiveness for such a

thing. No, lie still!" For she had tried to sit up. "There is naught to be gained by taxing your strength too far."

"But I must go home!" She struggled into a sitting position, clasping a hand to her head. "If my absence were discovered——"

"You cannot go yet," he interrupted in a tone of finality. "You are not equal at present to so long a walk, and if I bear you home on horseback we are bound to be discovered. Moreover, storm-clouds have now hidden the moon, and 'tis so dark you could not see a hand's-breadth before you." He took her by the shoulders and pressed her gently back upon the cushions. "I give you my word I will plague you no more with talk of marriage. Now rest for a while, and I will rouse you at first light."

She obeyed because to protest further seemed to demand too great an effort, and because she was practical enough to recognize the truth of what he said. He picked up her cloak from the floor and spread it over her, and then turned away to gather up the scattered papers from the table. While he locked them away in a cupboard and then took up the candles and the box of jewels, Charity lay with closed eyes. He paused by the day-bed and she sensed that he was looking down at her, but she did not dare to open her eyes for fear of what he might read in them. She remained motionless, as though she had fallen asleep, until she heard him go softly from the room and close the door. Then she rolled over on to her face and wept the most bitter tears she had ever shed, stifling the sound of her despair in the musty cushions.

7

The Accusers

She came back to the Moat House in the first grey light of a sultry dawn, when the clouds hung low and heavy and the very air seemed like a burden. Darrell had come with her to the brook below the woods, but she would not allow him to accompany her farther lest someone should see them together. He let her go reluctantly, and she went from him down the steep bank and across the thread of water which trickled along the brook's stony bed. When she looked back he was still watching her from the edge of the trees, but it seemed to her that an immeasurable distance already lay between them.

The house was still and silent as she let herself in by the stableyard door, but she knew that the servants would soon be stirring. Creeping into the nursery, she lay down fully dressed on the bed, for she felt utterly exhausted and the merciless pain was still thudding in her head. The room was unbearably hot and stuffy, and she lay in a kind of stupor, neither sleeping nor waking, while her thoughts roamed erratically among recent happenings. She was unaware of the passing of time, and returned to full consciousness of her surroundings only when the little boy came to stand beside her and tug at her arm. She roused then with a start, realizing, from the sounds in the house around her, that her usual hour of rising was already past.

In dismay she struggled to her feet, and, brushing aside with less than her usual patience the child's curious questions, hurried him into his clothes. Then, picking him up in her arms, hastened towards the hall where family prayers were held each morning for the entire household, and from which only severe indisposition was an acceptable excuse for absence.

When she reached the head of the staircase she could hear Jonas's voice already leading the prayers, and knew that she was even later than she had supposed. It was unthinkable that she should interrupt him, but since she did not dare to absent herself altogether she retraced her steps, went down the backstairs, and slipped unobtrusively into the hall through a door behind the most inferior servants. She knelt down among them and bowed her head, little Darrell beside her, but not before she had seen Jonas cast a boding glance in her direction.

While the interminable prayers continued she knelt there, not hearing what was said, unable even to find comfort, as she usually did, in her own private devotions. She was conscious only of weariness, of her throbbing head, and of a depression which seemed to weigh upon her as heavily and relentlessly as the stormy heat weighed upon the countryside. Once a low, distant rumble of thunder made itself heard, and the little boy huddled closer to her and slipped a hand into hers. He was terrified of thunderstorms.

At last the final words were said, and the assembled household rose and waited for Jonas, his mother and sister to leave the hall and so signify that the rest were free to go about their various duties. The signal did not come. Jonas craned his neck to look towards the spot where Charity stood, and crooked an imperious finger.

"You choose a lowly place this morning, cousin!" His voice, harsh with the mockery he so often used towards her, made everyone look in the same direction. "Come hither to me."

With little Darrell still clinging to her hand, Charity went slowly forward, the servants moving aside to give her room. So Jonas intended to humiliate her by rebuking her for her lateness before them all. She hid the resentment she felt, and walked calmly towards him with her head held high.

"You came somewhat tardily to prayers this day," he remarked as she paused before him. "That is a thing I will not tolerate, as you should know by now."

"I ask your pardon, cousin." Somehow she kept her voice steady, and empty of all expression. "I was late in rising."

For a moment he pondered her in silence, a humourless mockery still lingering about his lips, his blue eyes bright with a malicious satisfaction which woke in her an uneasiness she scorned to show. She looked coldly back at him, knowing it irked him that she was tall enough to face him thus levelly, with no need to raise her eyes.

"I'll warrant you were!" He spoke deliberately, and loud enough for all to hear. "If you kept virtuously to your

190

own bed, mistress, you would perchance be readier to rise betimes."

She heard the gasp of astonishment and disbelief which rippled round the hall behind her, but so great was the shock of his words that the sound scarcely impinged upon her consciousness. She glanced quickly at her aunt and Sarah, and saw that to Elizabeth the accusation had come as no surprise. Not knowing what else to do, she looked again at Jonas.

"By what right, cousin, do you insult me so?" she demanded, and was pleased to hear her own voice clear and angry.

His eyes continued to mock her. "Be sure I do not accuse you without just cause," he said, and beckoned to his body-servant. "Come forward, Stotewood, and repeat what you have already told me. Let all present know that I do not lightly impugn my cousin's honour."

Daniel Stotewood came towards them, bowing obsequiously to Mrs Shenfield, but with undisguised satisfaction in his pale eyes as he looked at Charity.

"As your honour commands," he said, and turned to address the assembled household. "Last night 'twere too hot to sleep, and just after midnight I were leaning from my window above the stableyard when I heard a door open below and a dog growl. Then I saw Miss Charity hurrying across the yard towards the gate. It seemed passing strange that she should be abroad at that hour, so I followed her. She went to the Dower House."

A murmur among the other servants greeted this disclosure. For the most part they bore Charity no ill will, but such events as this all too rarely disturbed the monotonous tempo of their lives and now they waited with avid eagerness to learn what would follow. Stotewood, savouring to the full his momentary importance, went on:

"A light were burning in one o' the lower rooms. She tapped on the casement, and Sir Darrell Conyngton came and let her into the house. I saw 'em come into the room together, but with no delay Sir Darrell shut the window and drew the curtains close." He paused, but with a look and a shrug which spoke volumes. "So I came home, but I kept watch and so saw her come stealing back to this house as dawn was breaking."

In the tense, expectant silence which followed his story every eye was turned upon Charity, every ear strained to hear what answer she would make. While Stotewood was speaking she remained facing her accusers, so that only they, and Mrs Shenfield and Sarah, could see her face, but her head was still high, her shoulders proudly erect.

"Well, cousin?" Jonas prompted her in a taunting voice. "Have you nothing to say? Will you not even admit that I do not accuse you of wantonness without due cause?"

Charity recovered slowly from the stunned dismay with which she had listened to Daniel Stotewood's accurate account of her visit to the Dower House. She knew it was useless to deny it. Even if the man had been lying, Jonas would still have accepted his word in preference to hers.

"I did go to the Dower House last night," she said steadily at length, "but I deny the evil insinuations you make. I had need to speak with Sir Darrell, and no other opportunity offered. My days are too fully occupied, Jonas, for me to have time to go abroad."

"Are they so?" he replied with heavy sarcasm. "And you would have us believe that what you had to say to Conyngton occupied you both till dawn? I counsel you,

192

cousin, not to add the sin of falsehood to that of wantonness. No woman goes to a man's house secretly by night unless he be her lover."

Charity pressed her hand to her aching head, trying to think clearly. She could not tell whether Jonas really believed his own accusations or whether he made them merely to shame her, but his last statement was unanswerable unless she betrayed the secret of the Conyngton jewels. To do that was unthinkable. Jonas would never rest until he had found some means of depriving Darrell of so valuable an asset. Beside her, the little boy clung tightly to her hand and whimpered softly. Though he did not understand what was being said, the tone of Jonas's voice was enough to tell him that all was not well.

"If you believe that of me, Jonas," she said scornfully at length, "it but betrays the evil which, for all your professions of godliness, festers in your mind. You forget, it seems, that Darrell Conyngton and I have been as brother and sister."

The smile faded from her cousin's face and sudden rage glittered in his eyes, for nothing angered him more than any aspersion against the sincerity of his religious beliefs.

"I do not forget, though, how long ago that was," he said furiously. "Would you have me believe 'tis as a brother you regard him now?" His hand shot out and closed upon her shoulder; his heated countenance was only a few inches from her own. "Well, cousin, do you? Answer me!"

Charity turned her head abruptly away, fearful that he would read the truth in her eyes, for his words were like a hand laid roughly upon the fresh wound of her own self-knowledge, so recently and painfully acquired. She felt the hot colour surging up into her face, and no effort of will, however desperate, could stay it. He laughed, harshly and triumphantly.

"Mistress, your blood betrays you! It answers me though you will not!" His hand on her shoulder swung her round to face the gaping servants. "If any of you doubted her shame, doubt it no longer! She bears the scarlet badge of guilt in her face!"

Startled by the sudden movement, the loud, hectoring tone of Jonas's voice, little Darrell began to scream in terror. Charity wrenched herself from Jonas's grasp and caught the child in up her arms, holding him tightly.

"Hush, my darling! Hush! There is naught to fear." He flung his arms about her neck and buried his face against her, still wailing with fright, and across his shoulder she looked with bitter anger at her cousin. "Abuse *me* as you will, Jonas, if it gives you satisfaction, but in God's name be man enough to refrain from bullying an innocent child!"

With a curse, Jonas seized the little boy by the waist and wrenched him forcibly from her arms, almost flinging him at the nearest maidservant. Ignoring his piercing screams, and grabbing Charity by the arm to prevent her from springing to his defence, he shouted at the startled woman:

"Take that squalling brat hence! Gather together such things as are his and bear him straightway to his father. I want him out of this house for good within the hour."

With a frightened, doubtful glance at Charity, the woman turned and bore her shrieking burden hastily up the stairs. Charity herself struggled unavailingly to follow.

"Loose me, Jonas! Let me go to him! God forgive you, he is almost beside himself with terror!" Then, finding anger vain, she fell to pleading. "Cousin, I beseech you! Send him hence if you must, but at least allow me to comfort him, to make him understand. 'Twill do him harm to be left in such a frenzy of fear. Aunt Elizabeth, for the love of pity tell Jonas that what I say is true!"

Mrs Shenfield shook her head. Her lips were tight-set, her eyes hard and bright with malice. "The boy has been pampered too much already," she said grimly, "and is a burden we shall be well rid of. There are more urgent tasks for you here, my girl, than the cosseting of Darrell Conyngton's sickly babe."

"There are indeed, madam," Jonas agreed unpleasantly, "but 'twill be no thanks to my cousin here if we are not burdened with another Conyngton brat ere many months be past!"

Charity turned on him like a fury, striking out with her free hand, but he caught her by the wrist and flung her aside so violently that she measured her length on the stone-flagged floor. Sarah cried out in anger and dismay and started to go to her aid, but was dragged back by her mother.

"Let her be!" Mrs Shenfield said sharply. "Your brother will deal with her as she deserves."

"My brother is a bully!" Sarah retorted recklessly. "A cruel, cowardly bully! If he believes this foul lie why does he not demand an answer of Sir Darrell, instead of browbeating a woman and a helpless child?"

There was a gasp of pleasurable horror from the servants, and a snigger, hastily stifled, for most of them remembered the outcome of Jonas's previous quarrel with Darrell Conyngton. Jonas himself turned slowly towards his sister, his face white now with a fury which had passed beyond heat.

"Get you to your bedchamber, Sarah," he said with ominous quietness, "and stay there until I give you leave to come forth. I shall have a word to say to you presently."

For an instant she hesitated, as though tempted to defy him, and looked anxiously at Charity, who had dragged herself up on a stool and now sat huddled there with her face hidden in her hands. Then she turned away, thrust past Daniel Stotewood, and went slowly and reluctantly up the stairs. Mrs. Shenfield nodded her satisfaction.

"That was well done," she said approvingly. "Sarah grows undutiful and stands in need of schooling." She nodded again, this time towards Charity. "What of this shameless slut? You would do well to turn *her* out of the house."

"What, so that she can shame us even further by going openly to her lover?" he said with a sneer. "No, madam, upon one thing I am resolved. She and Darrell Conyngton have met for the last time." He gestured to his servant. "Stotewood, bestow my cousin in some convenient place under lock and key until I have devised a fitting punishment for her. The rest of you go hence about your work, and let there be no time wasted in idle gossiping about this day's happenings."

Daniel Stotewood moved to Charity's side and grasped her arm, jerking her to her feet. Still dazed from the fall, she went with him unprotestingly, while the rest of the servants dispersed in various directions, preserving a discreet silence until they were out of earshot of Jonas and his mother. At the top of the staircase, where she had paused just out of sight, Sarah stood for a moment or two longer, biting her lip in anxious indecision. Then, turning, she sped through the upper part of the house, down the

196

backstairs and out through the stableyard. A few minutes later she was running as fast as her feet would carry her across the meadow in the direction of the Dower House, while the thunder rumbled closer and lightning stabbed the brooding clouds.

By the time she reached her goal she was nearly spent, her clothes clinging damply to her in the sticky heat, and the tale she gasped out to Darrell and to Henry Mordisford was breathless and disjointed. The two younger men, however, grasped the gist of it readily enough, though Mordisford looked faintly startled at the disclosure that Charity had been at the Dower House during the night.

"I pray you, Sir Darrell, go quickly to her aid!" Sarah concluded distractedly. "In his present humour there is no knowing what Jonas may do, and she has no one save you to protect her."

"Calm yourself, child! I go at once," Darrell said grimly, and looked at Mordisford. "Hal, do you ride with me?"

"Of a surety I do! What Miss Sarah has told us of Shenfield's treatment of my nephew gives me, I think, that right."

They rode headlong to the Moat House beneath a rapidly darkening sky. Sarah's story had aroused in Darrell a deep, implacable anger, but beneath the anger was a scarcely acknowledged fear that they might come too late. Jonas, in the grip of blind fury, was capable of any violence, as the wanton destruction of Conyngton bore witness. Darrell, spurring his horse along the road past his ruined home, remembered a summer day years before when he had chanced upon Jonas cruelly tormenting a little girl, a dark, dishevelled elf of a child who defended herself valiantly and yet was helpless against the superior strength of her tormentor. How different and yet how similar was the situation now.

Sarah, mounted on the crupper of Darrell's horse, was too concerned on Charity's behalf to feel alarm at their furious pace or apprehension of the punishment which might be hers for daring to fetch him. When the horses came to a plunging halt before the house it was Hal who lifted her down, for Darrell leapt from the saddle as though he had forgotten her and went to hammer furiously upon the door. He brushed past the startled servant who opened it, and with Hal and Sarah at his heels strode through the screens into the hall. At the same moment Jonas, drawn by the noise of their arrival, entered from the direction of the parlour, and so the two men confronted each other for the first time in more than five years.

It was dark in the hall, darker now by far than when Sarah had left it. The high, timbered roof was lost in shadow, the staircase rose into upper dimness, but Jonas Shenfield had no difficulty in recognizing the man who had just entered. Fury which had in it something of fear engulfed him, for this arrival took him unawares, and in his usual fashion he took refuge in bluster.

"You lack nothing in insolence, Conyngton, that you thrust yourself into this house after what has passed, but since you are come, you may take your son hence with you. I am prepared to house him no longer."

"Be sure that I shall take him!" Darrell's voice sounded oddly quiet after Jonas's hectoring tones, but it was a cold quietness, deadly as steel. "And not him alone. Where is Charity?"

Jonas uttered a short laugh and came farther into the hall, swaggering a little. He might fear Darrell Conyngton physically, but where Charity was concerned he was very sure of his ground. With his father at the point of death, he was head of the family, and his authority over her was indisputable.

"Where she may or may not be, my friend, is no concern of yours, for you and she have met for the last time. No matter how sinful, she is still my kinswoman, and it is my duty to protect her from one so obdurate in the ways of evil."

There was a little silence after his voice had ceased. A sudden flicker of lightning filled the hall for an instant with dazzling brilliance, clearly revealing the two men who faced each other there: sombre, crop-headed Puritan and elegant Cavalier. Elizabeth Shenfield had followed her son from the parlour, and to her there was menace in Darrell's tall, motionless figure. She moved quickly forward, saying fretfully to the lingering curious servant:

"Lights, you dolt! Bring candles! Must we peer at each other in darkness simply because 'tis morning by the clock?"

The man, prompted to speedy action by her tone, made haste to obey, but for Darrell and Jonas the interruption might never have occurred. At last Darrell said, still in that cold, deadly voice:

"Hypocrite! Damned, canting hypocrite! Your aspersions against Charity's honour are as false as hell, and you know it. I demand to see her!"

"Demand?" Jonas laughed again, revelling in this opportunity of baiting the man he so bitterly hated. "This is strange language to her guardian from a man who has seduced a foolish girl. By what right, I wonder, do you make that demand?"

The servant was lighting the candles which were set in sconces around the walls, the golden light growing to dispel the darkness of the storm. Darrell took a couple of paces forward until only a yard or two separated him from Jonas.

"I will tell you by what right," he said grimly. "I intend to marry her."

Jonas's mouth opened, but no sound emerged. A sickly pallor overspread his face, and his eyes blazed with such fury that even Darrell, expecting the most violent opposition, was startled. For a moment, he thought, the man looked almost insane. Then, after several fruitless attempts, Jonas gave strangled utterance.

"Marry her? You would wed that pert, penniless, shameless wench? My God! The mere thought is an affront to the pure and shining memory of your wife!"

As soon as the words were uttered he regretted them. Still glaring up at the tall man confronting him, he saw astounded comprehension leap into the hazel eyes, and knew that his jealously guarded secret was his own no longer. Darrell said very softly:

"My wife's name has no place on your lips, Shenfield, just as Charity has no place in a house where she is so slighted and misused. Now will you bring her to me, or must I go in search of her?"

A spasm of fury twisted the other man's face, and he put up a shaking hand to tug at his collar. "Not now, damn you, or ever!" he said viciously. "And if you seek to go beyond this room I will have my servants cast you from the house."

"Will you so?" Darrell still spoke quietly, but he moved with a swiftness which took Jonas unawares, and seized him by the throat, swinging him round and pinning him against the massive table in the middle of the hall. Jonas was powerfully built, but he was no fighting-man, and struggle though he might, he could not break free. The blood pounded in his head and his vision began to blur, and still the strong fingers at his throat exerted their relentless pressure.

"Where is she, Jonas?" Darrell's voice was as merciless as his hands. "Tell me, and spare yourself further hurt, for, as God is my witness, I will see her this day if I have to kill you first!"

"Sir Darrell, stop! Have you run mad?" Mrs Shenfield awoke from her horrified stupefaction and started forward. "Loose my son! I will fetch the girl to you!"

She ran from the hall, and Darrell released his victim and stepped back. Jonas sank to his knees by the table, his arms outspread across it, his forehead resting against its edge, his shoulders heaving as he fought to recover his breath. His hoarse, rattling gasps were the only sounds to break the silence, the heavy, brooding hush where for the moment even the thunder had ceased.

Charity, released with no explanation from the small, bare room where Stotewood had imprisoned her, supposed that she was being summoned to face whatever punishment Jonas had devised. Her head still throbbed unmercifully and she was stiff and aching from her fall, but her thoughts were wholly concerned with the child. Elizabeth thrust her into the hall and then brushed past her to go to Jonas, but Charity halted dazedly on the threshold. Then, catching sight of Darrell, ran forward with outstretched hands.

"Heaven be praised that you are here! Jonas took little Darrell from me by force, and he was so frightened! Oh, where is he? I must go to him!"

Sarah, who all this while had remained just within the

201

hall, standing close to Hal as though for reassurance, came quickly forward.

"I will fetch him," she said. "He must be somewhere abovestairs with Betsy. Bide here, Charity, and I will bring him to you."

She ran across the hall and up the stairs. Darrell, still holding Charity's hands tightly in his own, said gently:

"Little one, how is it with you?"

The concern in his voice and eyes brought a tinge of colour into her white cheeks, and she looked quickly away to where Elizabeth, having helped Jonas to the big chair by the fireplace, was hovering anxiously about him.

"I am well enough," she said in a low voice, "but I do not understand how you come to be here."

"Your cousin Sarah had the wit to fetch me, but do not vex yourself over that at present. Come, sit down."

He led her to a seat, and Hal came across to join them, while Jonas, slumped in his chair, fingered his bruised throat and looked venomously at Darrell. After a minute or two Sarah came running down the stairs again. The little boy was not with her, but one of the serving-maids followed at her heels, and Charity, recognizing the woman who had been given charge of the child, rose to her feet again with a chill premonition of disaster. Sarah looked from her to Darrell with dismayed and puzzled eyes.

"He has disappeared," she said breathlessly. "Betsy and the others have been searching the house, but he is nowhere to be found."

"I felt sure he was wi' Nurse," Betsy put in, anxious to exonerate herself, "but seems she were called to look to the master. I were putting together the little lad's clothes and such, as Master Jonas bade me, and by the time 'twere done he'd vanished clean away."

Another brilliant flash of lightning stabbed into the room, its brightness dimming the candlelight, and Charity clutched at Darrell's sleeve.

"We must find him!" she said urgently. "Poor mite, he is terrified of thunderstorms! After all the rest 'twould be enough to turn his reason if he were left alone during this one."

"We shall find him, never fear!" Darrell laid his hand briefly over hers in a gesture of reassurance. "The house must be searched again, more thoroughly, and the stables and other outbuildings also. You, girl! Summon the other servants and bid them lose no time about it, while the rest of us seek him in the garden. If he is out of doors he must be found before the storm breaks." He turned to Jonas, and now his voice was as cold as ice. "This is your doing, Shenfield! I counsel you to pray that no harm befalls my son."

He followed Charity, who, with Hal and Sarah, had already hurried out of the house, while Betsy went scurrying off in a different direction, calling to the other servants. Alone in the hall, Jonas and his mother looked at each other in appalled silence.

"The boy was still in our charge," Elizabeth said slowly at last. "What if some harm does befall him, and his father calls you to an accounting? It would please him well, and that sly wanton also, to force you again within reach of his sword."

"Think you I do not know it?" Jonas retorted savagely. "Though Conyngton is no fool, and must realize that he could not with impunity slay me. I have some influence now, while he, and those like him, are but our defeated enemies."

She regarded him uneasily. "Do you put your dependence upon that?"

He shook his head, heaving himself to his feet. "Only in the last extremity! Come, Mother, we had best busy ourselves also about this search, and if it falls to me to find the plaguey brat I warrant you it will go hard with him."

8

So Valiant a Heart

For years after that day Charity was to be tormented by nightmares in which she lived again that frantic search, although in waking moments only disjointed fragments of it remained in her memory. Late roses, red as blood against an old stone wall; the sundial with its grim, carven legend warning the world of the transience of life; lightning that ripped the sagging clouds, and the curiously expectant hush which preceded each deafening thunderclap.

At last, how soon or how late she could not tell, she found herself standing alone at the entrance of the tower. Reason told her that the steep, worn spiral stair was too arduous a climb for infant legs, and yet a hideous, compelling fear drew her within and up the steps, calling the child's name on a reassuring note which belied her sick anxiety. No answer came, and in the gaping maw of the tower far below no small figure lay huddled among the heaps of broken masonry and the thrusting weeds. Weak with relief she turned to retrace her steps, and so caught a glimpse, through one of the slit-like windows, of the great willow tree at the far end of the moat.

She stopped short, staring at it, for surely there was a slight movement of the graceful branches, although elsewhere every leaf hung motionless in the sullen air? With a swift renewal of hope she hastened down the stair and, reaching the doorway of the tower, saw Darrell a short way off, and beyond him, Hal and Sarah coming together along one of the paths. She waved to indicate the new direction of her search, but did not wait to see if they followed. Instead she went hurrying past the tower and along the water's edge towards the willow.

She had reached the hawthorn trees when she realized to her dismay that someone else was before her, for Jonas was walking towards her from the other end of the pool. He was peering about him and so did not see Charity in the shadow of the hawthorns, and before she could emerge from it he reached the willow tree and passed beneath its trailing branches. There was a shrill scream, and then he appeared again, dragging the little boy by one arm.

Charity cried out and broke into a run, but her voice was drowned by a rolling peal of thunder. Little Darrell, transformed by terror into a struggling writhing fury, was kicking and pummelling his captor, and with horror she saw Jonas wrench off one of the supple willow branches and bring it down hard across the child's back. She cried out again, in angry protest, and this time her voice reached him, for he checked with arm upraised and looked towards her. Dismay at her presence made him slacken his grip, and the child broke free and fled in panic towards her. Blind panic, which took no heed of her warning cry, of the glass-smooth water waiting so near, or tangled grass which tripped small, stumbling feet. She raced desperately forward, but in vain, and her scream of horror as he plunged into the pool rang piercingly across the garden beyond the wall.

After that one cry Charity's reaction was swift and instinctive. She was incapable of pausing to consider her own safety, or the chances of success, when little Darrell was struggling frantically in the water only a few feet from the bank, his small face contorted with terror. Without hesitation and without thought she plunged in after him, and her desperately groping fingers found and clutched a fold of his holland smock.

But the banks of the pool sloped steeply, and Charity had never learned to swim. The water closed over her head, and though when she fought her way to the surface again she saw that Jonas had flung himself down on the grass and was holding the tough willow branch out towards her, the end of it was beyond her reach. She sank again into the dark and choking depths, her last conscious thought that she must hold fast to the no longer struggling child.

The next thing of which she was aware was sickness and a painful, gasping fight for breath, of raindrops beating upon her face, and of the smell of grass and wet earth. She opened her eyes and found that she was lying on the ground beside the pool with her head in Sarah's lap. The rain was falling in a steady downpour, hissing across the meadows, and the whole storm-darkened scene eerily lit by flickering lightning and shaken by the roaring fury of the tempest now directly overhead. Memory returned with terrifying distinctness and she tried to raise herself, but Sarah's hands on her shoulders prevented it.

"Be still, dear coz!" Sarah's voice was low and shaken. "You are safe now."

"The child?" Charity gasped. "Sarah . . ."

"Sir Darrell brought you both from the moat. Lie still, love, I beseech you."

The raindrops were trickling down Sarah's cheeks—or were they raindrops alone? Gripped by dread, Charity tried once more to struggle up, and this time found an arm to lend her aid, and saw Jonas's pallid face bent over her. Beyond him, Darrell and Hal and Mrs Shenfield were kneeling on the grass, but even as she looked, Darrell rose slowly to his feet. His clothes were a sodden ruin, his hair hung lank and dripping about a stricken face, and in his arms the child lay motionless, limp as a broken puppet. Charity dragged herself to her knees and stretched out her hands towards him, but if he heard her broken cry he paid no heed. He seemed unaware of her, of any of them, as he stood staring down at the small lifeless body of his son. Despair engulfed her, and with it a swirling horror of darkness, so that she knew no more.

Thereafter, in a curious, disjointed way, she was aware of being borne into the house, of voices, hushed and grave, which murmured words she could not catch, and of hands that tended her, but it was not until some time later that she returned to full awareness of her surroundings. When she did she was lying in her bed in the old nursery, and Sarah was sitting beside her. The storm had passed, leaving behind it a grey stillness broken only by the whisper of falling rain, so that at first this seemed but an ordinary awakening and all that had gone before it an evil dream. Then she saw the narrow bed standing empty on the other side of the room, and Sarah with trembling lips and eyes reddened by weeping, and she knew that the nightmare was reality and that the child was dead.

For a time it seemed that Charity would die also. A high fever took her in its grip, and for days she wandered in a fearsome world of delirium, but through all the fevered fantasies that tormented her one picture remained constant, more terrible than any. The memory of Darrell standing stricken and unheeding beside the storm-lashed pool, with the body of his dead son in his arms. Even when the fever broke, and the other horrors faded and vanished, that remained, as though it had burned itself too deeply into her memory ever to be erased.

While she lay delirious, Sarah had caused the little bed to be carried away, and with it every other object which might serve to awaken memories of the child, but Charity had no need of material things to remind her of her loss. Sarah and old Nurse tended her with loving care, and even Elizabeth was strangely gentle on the few occasions she came to her bedside, but none of them could comfort her aching loneliness or guess at the agony of self-reproach which tortured her by day and night. Her recovery was slow, for the old zest for life was gone from her, and her defiant spirit no longer merely subdued, but broken.

Jonas, meanwhile, was deeming it prudent to tread warily, for though he had not intended the child's death and had even made some attempt to avert it, he was by no means certain that Darrell did not hold him responsible. During Charity's illness a kind of armed truce existed between them. While her life still hung in the balance Darrell was frequently at the Moat House, usually accompanied by Hal Mordisford, but Jonas kept out of their way and left Elizabeth to receive the guests. He would have liked to retreat to the greater safety of Plymouth, but stubbornness and vanity kept him in Conyngton St John.

At last, however, an urgent message from his uncle, demanding his immediate presence, furnished the excuse he was seeking. Charity's health was mending now, and Darrell came to the Moat House no more, merely sending his servant, John Parrish, each day to inquire how she did, but Jonas felt it necessary, before his departure, to make certain matters plain to her. He had reluctantly decided that for his own sake he must forgo the pleasure of punishing her, but she must understand that her escape was due solely to magnanimity on his part and that his authority over her was still absolute.

He found her lying on a day-bed in the parlour, while Sarah sat, sewing nearby. Jonas had not seen Charity since the accident, for this was the first time she had felt strong enough to leave her room, and he was startled by the change in her. Always slender, she now seemed like a wraith of her former self. Her clothes hung upon her, and in her face, where the faint, healthy colour had faded to the pallor of ivory, the fine bold contours of the bones showed plainly, but it was her listlessness which struck him with the greatest force. The patient, sorrowful droop of the lips, the indifference in dark eyes which had hitherto flashed scornful defiance even when she was outwardly at her most demure, struck him with an undeniable sense of shock, swiftly followed by satisfaction. This pale, meek young woman could not possibly be any longer a thorn in his flesh. She was tamed, subdued, brought to a proper state of humility and obedience.

"So, cousin!" he said patronizingly. "I rejoice to see

you so much recovered. Your health has given us all great cause for anxiety these past weeks."

The old Charity would have made some barbed retort, mocking him for the suggestion that he could ever feel anxiety on her behalf, but now his words did nothing to stir her from her lethargy. Even her voice was weary and lifeless as she said:

"I thank you, Jonas, I am well enough." She turned her head away, trying to check the uncontrollable quiver of her lips as she added in a lower tone: "Better, perhaps, if when I return."

"Cousin, such words display no proper spirit," he rebuked her pompously. "It has pleased the Lord to deliver you from death that you may use the gift of life thus bestowed upon you to His greater glory, and to atone for the sins and follies of the past."

He paused, but there was no change of expression in the pale, still face. It was almost uncanny, he thought, to see such emptiness where once all had been vitality and challenge.

"As your strength returns," he went on, "you will come to accept the truth of what I say. Endeavour to occupy yourself with some useful task, for idleness of mind and body breeds such impious thoughts. I go now to Plymouth. Let me find you in a more seemly frame of mind when I return."

Again he paused, and again she made no response. Jonas began to have the curious and uncomfortable feeling that he was talking to someone who was not really present. It irritated him, and when he spoke again annoyance was roughening his voice.

"Of the shame which you have brought upon yourself and upon this family I will say no more, save that I look to see you show a proper repentance, and by the blamelessness of your future conduct make amends for past transgressions. But mark this, Charity! You and Darrell Conyngton will meet no more. That I absolutely forbid."

This time she bowed her head, but whether in assent or merely to signify her understanding he could not be sure. It was Sarah, disturbed and greatly daring, who protested.

"How can it be possible, Jonas, for Charity and Sir Darrell to live within two miles of each other and never meet? Besides, he wishes to marry her."

"A pert tongue, Sarah, is an ill thing in a woman," her brother rebuked her sternly. "Remember that though I have chosen to overlook your deliberate flouting of my commands, it is not too late for your disobedience to be punished. Nor should you be foolish enough to believe Conyngton's fine talk of marriage. The only reason for that—if indeed it was honestly meant, which I doubt— was the child. Now that the child is dead, depend upon it that marriage will be mentioned no more." He turned to the door, adding over his shoulder: "I can waste no more time here in idle talk! While I am away you will both obey my mother in all things."

He went out, and Sarah, after one anxious glance at her companion, dropped her sewing and went to kneel beside the day-bed. Charity had turned her head away so that Jonas should not see her face. Her eyes were closed, but slow, painful tears trickled down her cheeks.

"Dearest, do not weep!" Sarah said urgently. "Jonas is cruel and wicked to distress you thus when you have been so ill, but he spoke only in malice. Pay no heed to him!"

"How can I not, when what he says is true? Ah yes, it is!" For Sarah had started to make an indignant protest. "I have known it ever since that dreadful day."

"I do not believe it! Why, everyone in the village knows the affection Sir Darrell has for you, and has had ever since you were both children."

"Ah, but you do not know! Sarah, it was *I* who persuaded him to stay in Devon! Do you suppose he can even think of me now with kindness, when but for me his son would still be alive?"

"Dear coz, how can you say so? Did you not come near to losing your own life trying to save the child?"

"Would that I had!" Charity's low voice was charged with desperation. "Ah, why did God not take me, and spare the babe?"

"Charity, listen to me! I was there when Sir Darrell brought you both from the pool, and I swear that his first thought was for you. And afterwards, when you were so ill, he was here day after day, although it cannot have been easy for him to come to this house when Jonas has so bitterly wronged him. There can be no doubt of the depth of his regard for you." She broke off, studying her cousin's face, and then with a little gesture of despair sat back on her heels. "You do not believe me!"

Charity shook her head, though she reached out to clasp the younger girl's hand. "I know that you seek only to comfort me, Sarah, but do not, I beg of you!" She pressed her free hand against her lips for a moment, trying to still their trembling. "No words, however kind, can take away the certainty that I am to blame."

"No words of mine, perhaps," Sarah said slowly, "but mayhap Sir Darrell himself could persuade you out of this folly. Could we not contrive——"

"No!" The refusal came sharp and high as Charity raised herself from the cushions. "Sarah, I forbid it! I refuse to see him!" She sank back again, and a sob broke from her lips. "How can I ever face him again with that dead innocent between us?"

Sarah was unconvinced, but her cousin's too brilliant eyes, and the flush which had risen to her hitherto pallid cheeks, warned her against pursuing the matter further. She set herself instead to soothe and comfort, believing that as Charity recovered she would come to view the tragedy more calmly, and to see that no blame for it attached to her.

Yet Charity's attitude did not change. She grew a little stronger, but as her health improved it seemed that her determination grew also. Many times Sarah tried to broach the subject of a meeting with Darrell, and each time she rejected it, more calmly than at first but with even greater finality. It was the only matter in which she showed any spirit at all.

For the rest, she remained sunk in the despair which had engulfed her at the time of the accident, and which had bred in her a vast indifference. It meant nothing that her aunt's brief kindness had passed and that her own persistent listlessness brought forth many a sharp rebuke. She knew that Hal Mordisford was still at the Dower House and that he and Sarah were meeting secretly, but could not rouse herself sufficiently to utter either protest or warning. She, to whom life had once seemed a thing of beauty and of challenge, found it now a wearisome burden, and shrank from the thought of the empty years stretching endlessly ahead, for what could the future hold for her save loneliness and sorrow? Already she felt but half alive, living through long, meaningless days and nights where nothing was real but the dull weight of grief.

On a day in early autumn she was sitting at the spinning-wheel in the parlour, but as so often happened now, her hands lay idle in her lap, her eyes gazed blankly before her. All day the thought of Conyngton had been in her mind, for she had dreamed the previous night of the manor as it used to be, and the awakening to harsh reality had brought with it a pain too cruel to be long endured. Suddenly she felt that the walls of the room were pressing like a heavy weight upon her, and that the Moat House was a prison in which she was trapped with no hope of release. She thrust her work aside and went out of the house, across the stableyard, and into the park.

It was a grey day, not cold, but with a dampness in the air which was a little more than mist, and a little less than rain; a day of silence and empty fields and falling leaves. This was the first time since her illness that Charity had been farther than the walled garden, but now she turned sharply away from the moat upon which she still could not bring herself to look, and walked slowly but steadily towards the brook. The climb up the steep hill beyond taxed her almost to the limit of her strength, but she scarcely paused when she reached the top. Like a sleepwalker she crossed the park and passed under the arch of the gatehouse.

On that cheerless day the ruined manor seemed more desolate than ever. A few late flowers still bloomed here and there in the tangled gardens, but already the first frosts of winter had touched the countryside with the chill threat of decay. Leaves were crimson and brown and gold, but in the damp, misty air their colours were muted; none of the pagentry of autumn was in evidence, but only its sadness, the sense of a year grown old, and slowly dying.

As she had done once before, Charity went up the terrace steps and on into the empty space which had once been the Great Hall of the mansion. The broken flagstones were damp beneath her feet and slippery with fallen leaves, and all around her the smoke-blackened walls reared up gaunt and forbidding. She sat down on a huge slab of fallen masonry and looked drearily about her. Here had been the vast fireplace where in winter whole tree-trunks had blazed, casting a warm, flickering glow over carved panelling and rich tapestry, glinting on ancient weapons adorning the walls. There the archway giving access to the Grand Staircase, and there the Minstrels' Gallery. For a moment, with a clarity which was part memory and part delusion, she saw Conyngton as it had once been, warm and welcoming and peopled with dear, familiar figures; felt again the sense of happy security, the joyous certainty of being loved, which had always enfolded her whenever she set foot within its walls. Then abruptly the vision faded and she was alone again in the forsaken ruins. The faint, far whisper of remembered voices was no more than the cry of a bird, the beloved forms a trail of mist, a silently falling leaf.

A sense of utter desolation possessed her. They were gone, lost beyond recall, the loved friends and the happy days. Life could not be faced without a purpose, and strength and courage ebbed away when there was nothing left for which to strive. This was the thought which had lurked unrecognized in her mind for many weeks, the truth which today she had come to Conyngton to find. Yet, bitter though it was, the knowledge brought with it a kind of peace. Slowly she let herself sink forward until she lay prone across the rough, damp stone, her head resting on her outstretched arms. This, after all, was where she belonged.

Time ceased to have any meaning, and it might have

been a minute later, or an hour, when she was roused by the sound of a footstep on the terrace, and Darrell's voice, sharp with anxiety, calling her name. She started up in incredulous dismay, and turned her head to see him coming quickly towards her through the shattered Hall. She put out her hand as though to ward him off but he dropped to one knee beside her and gripped her by the shoulders, and she saw that his face was white with shock.

"Charity!" he said again, his voice low and shaken. "Dear God in Heaven, I thought ... ! You lay so still!" He paused, and with a perceptible effort controlled his voice. "Little one, what do you here?"

She was trembling violently and it was several moments before she was sufficiently in command of herself to reply, but then she said in a breaking voice: "Do not ... be kind to me, Darrell. I know how you must regard me, but, believe me, you can blame me no more bitterly than I blame myself."

"Blame you?" he repeated gently. "Sarah told me of this foolishness, but, as I live, I scarcely credited it till now! Knowing you as I do, I could believe that you might reproach yourself for some fancied neglect, but not that you could ever suppose *I* would do so."

She turned her head away, the tears which since her illness had come so often welling up again in her eyes. "But the fault was mine! Had I not persuaded you to stay he would still be alive! Alison's child—so like her—and you loved her so dearly! Now you have nothing left, nothing at all!"

"Listen to me, Charity," Darrell said quietly. "I grieve for the boy—how could I not? He was my son! Yet I was a stranger to him, and even his mother is now no more to me than a sweet, fading memory. Yes, I loved her ..."

For Charity had looked quickly towards him, her lips already parted to protest. "I loved her gentleness, her beauty, her dependence upon me. The marriage was not of my choosing, but I was happy in it. Yet even during those first months of war, whenever I dreamed of Conyngton, then, waking or sleeping, it was your face I saw, not Alison's."

She made a little gesture of dismissal. "You and she had been married so short a time! Here at Conyngton I had been part of your life for years."

"So I told myself, yet as time went by her memory faded and grew dim, while yours remained as bright as any star. My steadfast star, to draw me home again at last! There was never a moment, Charity, when thought of the future did not mean also thought of you."

He paused and rose to his feet, taking her gently by the arms and lifting her up also. Looking up into his eyes, she read there not the accusation and reproach which she had dreaded to see, but something deeper by far than the old, careless affection.

"It is time for truth between us," he went on, "truth which would have been better spoken that night at the Dower House. I love you, Charity! It was not your persuasions, your talk of duty and accusations of pride which kept me here in Conyngton St John, although my mind recognized the justice of your words. No, you said something else that morning, and it spoke not to my mind but to my heart. 'I will not go,' you said, and I knew then that I could not go either. That I was bound to you by the strongest chains this world can forge." He put his arms around her and held her tightly and spoke with his lips close to her tear-wet cheek. "You say that I have nothing left, but you are wrong, my little one! You are my hope, my strength, my very life, and while I still have you I have all the world."

She had listened to him with a wonder so great that it was almost disbelief, and though still enfolded in his arms and with her head against his shoulder, said in a low voice:

"It cannot be true! Such happiness as this can come only in dreams."

"My poor love!" Darrell's voice was very gentle. "You have known too much of loneliness and sorrow, and faced it with so valiant a heart. But never alone again, my dear one! Whatever the future holds we face it together."

"Together!" she whispered. "Ah, Darrell, how can that ever be? That we love each other alters nothing—Jonas will never consent to our marriage. He has forbidden me ever to see you again."

"Yet you are here," he reminded her with a smile, "safe in my arms. Believe me, little one, it was not Jonas's commands which kept me from you all these weeks, but only the knowledge that you refused to see me. When I learned of that I knew doubt indeed! I remembered how distressed you seemed that night when I spoke of marriage, and feared that you had so long regarded me only as friend and brother that you shrank from the thought of becoming my wife."

She shook her head. " 'Twas because I no longer regarded you thus that I was afraid. I could not marry you, believing that your love still belonged wholly to Alison. I was jealous of her, Darrell, and so bitterly ashamed of my jealousy. Then after . . ." Her voice faltered for a moment, but she steadied it determinedly. "After the accident so much more seemed to stand between us——"

"Nothing stands between us," he broke in firmly.

"Nothing save Jonas's enmity, and that, God aiding us, we shall find the means to overcome. Little one, I have been near desperate all this while, knowing that you were torturing yourself so needlessly and being unable to come to you, to bring you comfort! When Sarah told me today that I would find you here——"

"Sarah told you?" she interrupted. "How could she know it?"

"She saw you set out, and came after you. It seems she thought at first that you were bound for the Dower House, and followed only because she feared your strength would not be equal to the walk. When she realized that you were coming here instead she grew frightened and hastened to tell me of it." He looked curiously at her. "Charity, why *did* you come?"

She was silent for a moment, ashamed now of the despair which had brought her to Conyngton, but she was incapable of lying to him. "Because I felt that I could endure no more," she said at length in a low voice. "All I had ever known of true happiness lay here, and since I thought that all happiness was beyond my reach for ever, it seemed that this was the only fitting place for me. Here, where all joy and hope and beauty lie in ruins."

He remembered how still and quiet she had lain across the stone when he found her, and a chill hand seemed to touch his heart. If Sarah had not followed her how long would it have been before anyone thought to seek her here, in the ruined manor which stood forsaken now from year to year?

"No," he said quietly, "it is only a house that lies in ruins, my love. A fair house, and one very dear to both of us, but Conyngton is more than brick and stone and carven wood. It is honour and duty, and the love of all those who have gone before us and those who will come after. These things cannot be destroyed. And one day the house itself will rise again, as beautiful as before. It may not be granted to us to see it, but one day it *will* be rebuilt, if not by us, then by our children, or our children's children."

"Ah, if I could believe that!" Charity lifted her head and looked at the desolation all around them. "To know that this was not the end——"

"You must believe it," he said gently, and took her chin in his hand, turning her face towards him. "Just as you must believe that nothing in this world can sunder us from each other. It will not be easy, little one! There will be times of doubt, and a need for patience and for faith which may try us both to the limit of endurance, but somehow, some day, we shall belong wholly to each other. If you love me as greatly as I love you, then we shall find the way."

Looking down into her face, still pale and drawn from illness, and from a suffering which was more than physical, he saw a sudden radiance steal into it, as though she were awakening from long and troubled sleep.

"If I love you?" she whispered. She smiled at him, and the valiant, steadfast spirit was shining again in the dark eyes. "Dear heart, whatever else you doubt, be sure of that! Is not my life, my happiness, so close entwined with yours that nothing can sever them? Yes, you are right! Do Jonas what he will, he can never come between us now."

Dorothy Eden

Ms. Eden's novels have enthralled millions of readers for many years. Here is your chance to order any or all of her bestselling titles direct by mail.

☐ AN AFTERNOON WALK	23072-4	1.75
☐ DARKWATER	23153-4	1.75
☐ THE HOUSE ON HAY HILL	X2839	1.75
☐ LADY OF MALLOW	Q2796	1.50
☐ THE MARRIAGE CHEST	23032-5	1.50
☐ MELBURY SQUARE	22973-4	1.75
☐ THE MILLIONAIRE'S DAUGHTER	23186-0	1.95
☐ NEVER CALL IT LOVING	23143-7	1.95
☐ RAVENSCROFT	22998-X	1.50
☐ THE SHADOW WIFE	22802-9	1.50
☐ SIEGE IN THE SUN	Q2736	1.50
☐ SLEEP IN THE WOODS	23075-9	1.75
☐ SPEAK TO ME OF LOVE	X2735	1.75
☐ THE TIME OF THE DRAGON	23059-7	1.95
☐ THE VINES OF YARRABEE	23184-4	1.95
☐ WAITING FOR WILLA	23187-9	1.50
☐ WINTERWOOD	23185-2	1.75

Buy them at your local bookstores or use this handy coupon for ordering:

FAWCETT PUBLICATIONS, P.O. Box 1014, Greenwich Conn. 06830

Please send me the books I have checked above. Orders for less than 5 books must include 60c for the first book and 25c for each additional book to cover mailing and handling. Orders of 5 or more books postage is Free. I enclose $_____ in check or money order.

Mr/Mrs/Miss_____

Address_____

City_____ State/Zip_____

Please allow 4 to 5 weeks for delivery. This offer expires 6/78.

A-5

HELEN MacINNES

Helen MacInnes's bestselling suspense novels continue to delight her readers and many have been made into major motion pictures. Here is your chance to enjoy all of her exciting novels, by simply filling out the coupon below.

☐	ABOVE SUSPICION	23101-1	1.75
☐	AGENT IN PLACE	23127-5	1.95
☐	ASSIGNMENT IN BRITTANY	22958-0	1.95
☐	DECISION AT DELPHI	C2790	1.95
☐	THE DOUBLE IMAGE	22787-1	1.75
☐	FRIENDS AND LOVERS	X2714	1.75
☐	HORIZON	23123-2	1.50
☐	I AND MY TRUE LOVE	Q2559	1.50
☐	MESSAGE FROM MALAGA	X2820	1.75
☐	NEITHER FIVE NOR THREE	X2912	1.75
☐	NORTH FROM ROME	Q2441	1.50
☐	PRAY FOR A BRAVE HEART	X2907	1.75
☐	REST AND BE THANKFUL	X2860	1.75
☐	THE SALZBURG CONNECTION	X2686	1.75
☐	THE SNARE OF THE HUNTER	X2808	1.75
☐	THE VENETIAN AFFAIR	X2743	1.75
☐	WHILE STILL WE LIVE	23099-6	1.95

Buy them at your local bookstores or use this handy coupon for ordering:

FAWCETT PUBLICATIONS, P.O. Box 1014, Greenwich Conn. 06830

Please send me the books I have checked above. Orders for less than 5 books must include 60c for the first book and 25c for each additional book to cover mailing and handling. Orders of 5 or more books postage is Free. I enclose $_____ in check or money order.

Mr/Mrs/Miss_____

Address_____

City_____ State/Zip_____

Please allow 4 to 5 weeks for delivery. This offer expires 6/78.

A-8